The Black Widow of Hazel Green

ISBN **978-1-947514-43-0**

Printed in the United States of America
St. Clair Publications
P. O. Box 726
Mc Minnville, TN 37111-0726

http://stclairpublications.com

**Cover photo: Brenda Starr**

Cover Design Kent Grey — Hesselbein Design Studio

**www.kghdesignstudio.com**

# The Black Widow of Hazel Green

*A dark historic novel based on*

*a gruesome true story*

## Stanley J. St. Clair

Edited by Matthew Jackson

**StCP**

**Other historical works by Stanley J. St. Clair:**

*Prayers of Prophets, Knights and Kings;* History of Prayer, 2006, Trafford Publishing Co.

*Mysterious People of the Bible in the Light of History;* 2008, St. Clair Publications

*A Place in Time;* Reconstruction Era Novella, 2009, St. Clair Publications

*Conspiracy in the Town that Time Forgot;* True Crime Drama, 2009, St. Clair Publications

*Quinn;* Family Historic Novella based on a True Story, 2009, St. Clair Publications

*Beyond the Thistle Patch;* Memoirs of Youth, 2010, St. Clair Publications

*Turning Point at Gettysburg;* Civil War Historic Novel based on a True Story, 2021, St. Clair Publications

*They Call it Treason;* American Revolutionary War Historic Novel based on a True Story, 2021, St. Clair Publications

# *Acknowledgement*

My deepest gratitude to Mrs. Lori Christensen, owner/director of Cannon Dance Academy in Woodbury, Tennessee, for bringing this uncanny true story to my attention by a skit which she performed on 24 October 2021 at an event held at Warren Arts in McMinnville, Tennessee, where I was honored to be selected to represent Alexander Jeffries.

I began my study immediately thereafter, and it greatly surprised me that I could find no novel or motion picture about the bizarre life of Elizabeth Dale Gibbons Flanagan Jeffries High Brown Routt.

This novel emerged from much research. Of course a lot of it is conjecture. But it is woven around actual events in the lives of these real people.

**Parents strongly warned!**

*This book contains offensive racial slurs and vivid portrayals of violence and murder.*

# Chapter One

## 1968: Hazel Green, Alabama

It was late evening, October 6, 1968. The haunting hunter's moon peeked ominously through the dark, lacy clouds hovering over Northeastern Alabama. Halloween was fast approaching and mischief must commence.

Flames of scarlet, azure and amber leapt gaily from the smoldering remains of the "Haunted House of Hazel Green," atop an ancient sacred Indian mound. Two brick chimneys stood like solemn sentinels against the murky welkin above. The front brass door knob held a reddish glow as it fell limply to the hardened ground.

From a safe distance, behind the Wade smoke-house, two smudge-faced teenage hooligans sniggered insidiously at the glaring spectacle which they had proudly created. Surely history would applaud them for putting a glorious end to that God-forsaken tumbling old mansion. No one rushed in to extinguish the blazes. It seemed that no one really cared.

The Routt plantation mansion, in the ante-bellum era, had been a bustling center of social activity and whimsical balls. But now, all that remained of this period at Hazel Green were the haunting tales of a callous, avaricious woman, Elizabeth Dale Gibbons Flannigan Jeffries High Brown Routt, who was rumored to have viciously poisoned her husbands and buried more than a few of them there, beneath the cursed sod of that bleak plantation, over a hundred years earlier.

Children in Madison County had grown up cringing at ghost stories which had been passed down from one generation to the next. The tales came in various forms. Many were still afraid to walk, or even drive past the property, on what was now Joe Quick Road, at night; even this long after the frightful saga had come to a sudden halt, immediately before the onset of the Civil War.

Was the land under a curse because Alexander Jeffries had chosen this hallowed spot to build a log cabin as a dignified perch from which to observe his cotton plantation in 1818? What specters awaited trespassers there?

He had purchased 500 acres in two separate tracts from Archibald Peterson and Thomas Murphy. He had then obtained slaves, as needed, from the arrogant Thomas McCrary, down the road to the south, at Three Forks of Flint. McCrary had boasted to everyone that he owned the largest mass of slaves in the entire county.

Jeffries had driven his subservient workers as much as 16 hours a day. First there was the arduous task of clearing over a hundred acres of his land, then planting a fresh cotton crop each spring, meticulously pruning it, watering it and harvesting it each fall. Cotton was king—the predominant cash crop. The invention and manufacturing of the cotton gin had strength-ened the use of slaves because cotton could be produced much faster than in the past. Alexander Jeffries had developed into one of the most significant cotton producers in the entire region.

Alabama had become a state in 1819; Huntsville had been chosen as its temporary capitol and Madison County was the center for cotton growth.

In the flat area behind the mound he had also built sprawling stables which were filled with pricy horses for riding, plowing and pulling the wagons and surrey. Among them were sleek, staunch Arabians and elegant, graceful Tennessee Walkers.

Did the ghosts of the Natives buried there cry out for revenge? Some claimed that the spirits of the ancient Indians roamed freely over the consecrated mound on the darkest of nights.

Or could it have been a more recent miscarriage of human rights which had caused the house and land to be so dreadfully blighted?

Though the choice of the building site could easily have been a harbinger of Jeffries' final woes, something jarringly more damning had been brewing.

The spirit of a woman in a sheer black gown, many swore, could be seen and felt in the dead of night, hovering over the crumbling grave stones behind the dilapidated manor.

But to even attempt to comprehend the events that had happened at Hazel Green, and why, we need to learn what made Elizabeth who she was.

To set the stage, we must travel further back in time—much further.

# *Chapter Two*

## 1797: Snow Hill, Maryland

**T**he early April morning held a crisp promise of excitement for 29-year-old Adam Dale. As he gazed pensively out the window of his Maryland home, his ears were greeted by the piercing Mew-calls of a majestic flock of gulls dotting the sandy beaches of the nearby Worcester coast.

His much-loved little family was still sleeping peacefully. Shutting out the wailing cries, Adam's thoughts began rapidly spinning back over his adventuresome past. An awfully lot had happened to bring him to this crucial crossroads in life.

He could still remember his childhood as if it were yesterday. He first reflected on how he had impatiently awaited the arrival of his 14th birthday so that he would be permitted to follow in his father's footsteps. It meant the world to him to join the militia in the quest for American independence.

Yes, his father was his real hero. Lieutenant Thomas Dale had immigrated to New England from Londonderry, Northern Ireland as a young man. He had commanded two battalions of Minute Men in 1777 to protect a Whig outpost in Salisbury against a Tory uprising.

Adam deliberated on how he had impatiently pranced back and forth on the hardwood floor of his childhood home trying to determine how he was going to be able to raise a group of young boys to deter the progress of Lord Cornwallis when he marched through Maryland. His efforts had been highly successful, however, and he had earned himself a proud place in the history of America as a young teen.

His ruminations then flew forward to the marvelous day when he had married the beautiful Mary Hall of Sussex County, Delaware at his mature age of 21. He called her Polly, though. A smile of satisfaction rested on his thoughtful face.

Polly was from one of the most prestigious families in all of New England. But that didn't matter one little bit to him. He wasn't seeking fortune or fame. He was from noble ancestry, himself, though his parents never bragged of their heritage to him. He knew only from questioning his mother. His deep love and devotion for Polly was all that really mattered. Oh, how glad he was that he had taken her to wife! He truly believed that she was the best thing that had ever happened to him! She had been a truly devoted spouse and caring mother.

So far, they had brought four special children into this fledgling country that was being called Colonial America.

Suddenly his recollections were interrupted by a strange giggle emitting from the children's room. He smiled and shook his head, though there was no one there to see him. He knew beyond a shadow of a doubt which child it was. Only two-year-old Lizzie made such sounds.

Little Lizzie—Elizabeth Evans Dale—had been born in Worchester County, Maryland on 28 October 1795, just before All Hallows Eve, with a silver spoon planted firmly in her smug little mouth. There had just been something a bit different about her from the moment of her birth—you might even say peculiar.

Lizzie had been their third child. The oldest was a boy named Edward, who was often overly nervous, but healthy as a little horse and a good playmate for little Lizzie. The second had been another boy, Lemuel, who had come down with throat distemper and died at a very young age. Many years before, this would have been a common occurrence, as this mysterious disease had wiped out a generation of precious little ones in this section of the country. But the aftereffects of that terrible epidemic must have lingered, and as weak as the poor child was, it had taken roots in his feeble little body. Another son, Thomas, had come along that year.

Adam turned back toward the window and continued to nurse his memories.

These were the stories that his children would grow up hearing. His experiences would help form their characters if they would let them.

His family owned a sizable farm there in Snow Hill. He had gotten his start from his father. But the soil in Maryland was badly worn out by 100 years of farming.

Now he had been informed of fertile lands in the newly formed state of Tennessee in need of ambitious pioneers to settle there and develop the property. He had been assured that he would be granted a large section of it. Revolutionary soldiers were being given first choice, and he would receive 640 acres. His father, as a Second Lieutenant, would be granted 1,000 acres.

Though he would have to leave the only homeland he had ever known, he had no doubt what he must do. Of course he had no way of comprehending what would lie ahead, so he didn't know whether to laugh or cry. But the day to go forward had now come.

# Chapter Three

## October 1800: Smith County, Tennessee

**A** drifting, intermittent breeze and overhanging cumulous clouds had accompanied Adam that day. He had barely stabled his horse for the night when, in the dullness of twilight, he could make out the image of a lone rider approaching.

"Hey there, mister! I didn't know that there was anyone settlin' down here in this part of the country yet!"

Adam was relieved. His visitor was safe, like a friendly fire.

"Yes, sir! I'm the only one in these parts, though! My name's Dale, what's yours?"

"Yates, Earl Yates! Good to meet you, Dale! I rode down from Dixon Springs, a far piece to the north of here. I'm on my way to the new settlement at Rock Island. I've got a friend named William Martin who claimed some land down there on the river and I'm goin' to see how he's comin' along. Well, we all call the ole boy 'Rock' now! Do you have a family?"

"Yeah, but they're still up north where I came from. Maryland. I just finished getting my little house built here and I want them to come on down as soon as they can, but I don't know how to best get word to them. I suppose I'll have to ride over to Nashville to get a letter out. I hope they can make it before winter sets in good."

"Well, you're in luck, Dale! You won't have to go that far! They just opened a post office up at Dixon Springs the day before I left.

"It took me two days to get this far, but I cleared a good path so it shouldn't take you that long. You can go up there and send word straight away to your family!"

"Hey! That's great news, Yates!"

"By the way, do you have a little clean water I can get from you? My canteen's about dry! I'm awful particular about what I drink. Heard of a fellow getting' poisoned on bad water. I think something must have been killed in the creek up near where I live and left there. Probably poisoned. It may be Indians trying to run us off, just don't know. Didn't I pass a spring up there a bit?" Yates pointed.

"Sure did. I've got plenty of good water. But I'll do you one better, Yates, I'll cook us up some squirrel for supper! I shot a couple while I was picking corn today! They're a lot like those dad-burned blackbirds when it comes to stealing corn!"

"You got that right! Sounds good to me! I have a few biscuits wrapped up in a scrap of cloth here in my saddle bag. You can use 'em to make us some dumplin's!"

"I sure will! Come on in, Mr. Yates." Adam pulled the door open and motioned with his hand. "You can stay here tonight and we can both start out early in the morning!"

"Thank you! Don't mind if I do."

That night, lying on his pallet, it was harder than usual for Adam to get to sleep. His mind was always buzzing with what he wanted to do the next day when he went to bed. But tonight was different. Soon he was going to be able to have his family with him! Instead of thinking entirely about the next day, he replayed the last three years in his mind before he drifted off to dreamland.

Adam thought about how he had struck out alone on horseback with a sturdy pack horse carrying only the basic necessities. Things like his gun, cooking and eating utensils, a quilt, a hoe, an axe, and some seeds to start a garden and cornfield.

He remembered how he had gone through Virginia along the Great Valley Road which had taken him through the Cumberland Gap into Tennessee. Along the way he had stopped for a few more things that he knew he would need on the way and after he reached his property. Things like a short cane fishing pole, hammer, nails, hinges, an adz, a rope and candles. When he had reached the end of the Great Valley Road at Knoxville, he had taken the Nashville Road which had been created by the government in 1788, hunting and fishing as he went for his food. Many nights while camped, he had heard the chilling howls of wolves and peculiar, unknown splashing sounds in the rivers and creeks.

But what had really stuck in his most fond memories was the day he had finally reached the area of southern Smith County which would eventually become DeKalb County. He had found that the land was untouched and feral. The soil was incredibly rich.

He loved remembering how he had made a small shed of limbs in which to shelter his two horses. Adam had always cared highly about the protection of his animals. He had slept on the ground the first few nights on the east side of the horse shed which knocked off most of the wind typically coming from the west.

After walking out and staking off his allotted claim, he had thrown up a hovel near the edge of the jagged cliff overlooking Smith Fork Creek, which he called "Crooked River," for want of a better name, in which to live while he was preparing the land and building his home. Then he had dug a deep hole for a privy downwind a ways.

Everything he had done since his arrival was running through his busy mind that night.

After that he had cleared out a good sized spring which flowed into the creek to the north of the spot where he intended to build his house. Then there were the rails which he had split from young Chestnut trees to build the fence for a nice-sized lot for his horses.

Next, he had felled several tall poplar trees for logs and cut underbrush to form a large clearing; then chopped up the soil with his hoe and scraped out rows for a cornfield and a small vegetable garden. These were tasks which he knew would become regular annual chores.

All by himself, he had laid off the shape of the house, carefully placed stone piles for a foundation, built a fireplace of rocks calked with mud, and prepared and notched the logs. With the help of his strongest horse—his pack horse—and a rope, he laid the logs and built a sturdy two-room cabin with an attic. He had hewn boards with his adz, boxed the windows in and made shutters to close them off when the wind blew and when the weather turned frigid.

With this memory he finally began to get drowsy. At last he was able to settle down and get some restful sleep. His dreams were all of his precious family and the great life that was sure to come.

But Adam was so excited that he was up before 5:00 the next morning. He cooked them some mash for breakfast from meal that he had ground with a round rock from the creek and bid his visitor adieu.

He then scrawled out a letter to his darling wife:

*My Dear Polly,*

*I have found a land which flows with milk and honey, like the Promised Land in the Bible. I feel like a modern Abraham. This soil is very rich. There is a terrible lot of game here. I saw a buffalo the first day I was here and have killed some deer. I keep the meat in a spring house I made.*

*I have built us a fine little house and cleared several acres of the land. Please come as soon as possible and bring our family and any of our friends who still want to take part in this wonderful adventure with us.*

*I will be looking each day for your arrival. I miss you and our precious children so much I can't even begin to tell you!*

*If you will go to Nashville, Someone there can point the way to the east to get you to me. I have worked on this end to improve the road that comes here. There will be less steep mountains that way than along the Great Road that I came on. See you soon!*

*Your loving husband,*

*Adam*

He folded that precious piece of paper, sealed it with candle wax and hightailed it up to Dixon Springs. It only took him one long day to get there. The daylight hours were getting shorter, so by the time he arrived, it was pitch dark and the post office was already closed, so he camped for the night before taking the letter in to mail the following morning.

# *Chapter Four*

## December 1800: Smith County, Tennessee

As the Conestoga wagon caravan began to come into view, Adam was so anxious and wound up that his heart was throbbing a mile a minute. He found himself loping like a deer toward it, thinking only of his immense anticipation!

As soon as Polly had received Adam's letter, she had followed his instructions and passed the news along to his family and a large group of friends who had expressed an interest in joining them in their new exciting venture.

His father, Thomas; his mother, Elizabeth; his young brothers, Thomas, Jr. and teenaged John, his sisters, Martha and Sophia, plus a host of others had come. Forty souls in all had crammed into covered wagons and headed south as soon as they could get their goods packed and loaded. Some had teams of horses; others, oxen.

They had traversed through Pennsylvania, along the Ohio and Cumberland Rivers to Nashville, where they had stopped briefly, made sure they got on the right road and bartered for supplies and food.

Going had still been rough a good deal of the way, especially where they had found that the road had been badly washed by heavy rains and there were deep ruts to contend with. They had traveled along the Nashville Road east, which had taken them directly to Adam's granted land.

They arrived on Wednesday, December 24—Christmas Eve! This seemed like divine timing to Adam! The weather had not gotten really harsh yet and they were awfully happy about that fact!

When Adam reached Polly's wagon, he intuitively jumped aboard, gave her a long, loving kiss; grabbed Lizzie out of her lap and hugged her till she thought she would wet her clothes.

"Papa!" Lizzie squealed, "You're hurting me!"

Letting her down as gently as possible, he glanced up to see the other children rushing toward him. Little Thomas had been asleep in Edward's lap in the back of the wagon, but had awakened and both of the boys had come flying out to greet their papa! Well, of course Thomas couldn't move very fast, but he toddled out as best he could to meet his papa!

Adam was so elated to see his family that they all—except for the wee ones—sat up most of the night talking; literally "burning the midnight oil."

"What I have in mind," Adam told his brother Tommy, "is building a corn mill just north of here on Crooked River so that everyone will have a place to get their corn ground into meal when the time comes."

"That sounds really wonderful, Adam!" Tommy smiled. "Always planning ahead! John and I will be glad to help you!"

"Speak for yourself, brother!" the teen said as he ambled up with Adam's water dipper in his hand.

Adam knew that the wry smile on young John's lips was all in pure adolescent fun.

"Come on, John! Adam'll feed us well while we're working. And might even grind our whole family some corn without taking a toll! Won't you, bruv?"

"You betcha! I'd do that anyway!" Adam said with a smile, slapping Tommy on the back. "But it's Christmas time right now." Then his look got serious. "We'll talk more about that later. No need to start building till spring! Let's get some sleep and in the morning we can celebrate the birth of Christ!"

As Adam opened the door to let his family go back to their wagons at around 2:30, he could see that tiny snowflakes had begun to fall.

The next morning, the ground was barely covered, but it was still a white Christmas. The first one that Adam had seen since he had been in Tennessee.

Polly and some of the other ladies prepared a scrumptious breakfast in the cabin from eggs, sausage, flour and other food supplies that they had purchased in Nashville. And to Adam's delight, fresh coffee! Boy had he missed his morning coffee!

Everyone came dragging in, one by one, yawning and grunting. They had to eat in shifts. About 9:00 o'clock the earliest risers began gathering just outside the cabin to sing Christmas carols while their breath sent up freezing puffs into the sullen heavens.

That day the new residents parked their wagons in a large circle to use as their home bases until each family could claim land and build their own cabins. Adam had left a big open field in front of his house for this very purpose. His lot was crowded with the new horses and oxen and had to be enlarged. The newcomers would have to pitch in with cutting and splitting more rails.

During the next week, several of the other men helped Adam build a common fire pit, using large creek stones, in the center of the circle. It was needed for cooking and to keep the chill knocked off the camp. The perimeter would also serve as a community meeting place.

Adam began at once to try to teach them the survival techniques that he had learned by living there all of this time. But several of them laughed and told him that they had already learned them on their way there!

"You don't teach your granny how to suck eggs," Henry Burton told him. They both chuckled.

Adam held a meeting in the circle on New Year's Eve and spoke to the colony residents about his plans to build a town there.

"This place gives us all the liberty to be land-owners and carve out a place in history for ourselves and our posterity. We can be mighty proud of what we are doing for our country and the great new state of Tennessee! This land is very rich and we can grow fine crops here. New settlers will come in, but we are the first! No one can take that away from us!"

He heard cheery cries rising from within the assembly of "Hurray for Adam Dale!" and "Long live our brother!" Some whistled loudly, holding their fingers on their teeth.

Adam felt a slight frisson, but he made no outward response. He never wanted anyone to think of him as being egotistical or selfish. He wasn't a large man, but he had a big heart.

And so, Adam Dale founded the first town in what would later become DeKalb County, Tennessee, and named it Liberty.

But little Lizzie cried to be back by the ocean, where she could wiggle her tiny toes in the salty sand.

# Chapter Five

## 1801: Liberty, Tennessee

"**W**ell, the time has come," Adam told his younger brothers one cool evening near the first of April. "Tomorrow we start work on the mill!"

The days had been gradually warming and the harsh winds of March had given way to a calmer spring environment.

"Aw, shucks! Do we have to, Papa?" 15-year-old John grunted with a childish whimper. "Can't we pitch some more games of horseshoe first?"

Adam threw back his bushy head and guffawed.

"Do you want me to go get Papa to see what he says? If I was really your papa, I'd show you a thing or two! But since you're my baby brother and free labor, the least I can do is say, 'please!'"

Little John laughed and Tommy reached over and gave him a big brotherly hug.

So Adam and his brothers constructed a log mill on his property on Smith Fork Creek that spring. By the middle of June, the large mill wheel, which they had brought in from Nashville on a wagon, was turning with the rapid rush of the chilly water. The huge grindstone they had gotten at the same time was installed and ready for action. Life was a true pleasure and Adam felt a deep sense of personal accomplishment. That was important to him.

A friend of the Dales named Daniel Allen, a brother of Jesse, who was building a cabin on Eagle Creek, had taken up land nearby on Clear Fork, which flowed into Smith Fork Creek, that year. After getting a clear title, Daniel decided he would move farther west, so he sold his property to Adam's father, Thomas. Actually he traded it to him for a good work horse!

Thomas had been living with Adam while clearing his own land. His wife, Elizabeth, couldn't fathom what he had done! She just shook her head in sheer disbelief.

"What on earth do you need more land for, Mr. Dale?" You have so much already!"

"Well, Darling," he said, raising his left eyebrow, "the good Lord isn't making any more of it. Somebody will want it after I'm dead and gone."

His wife just shook her head some more and let out a long sigh.

Thomas, Sr., who clearly owned more property than anyone in the Liberty community, with the help of family and friends, soon built a two-story log home within walking distance of Adam's house. John loved it! He had his own room now!

Late that August, Adam's and Polly's daughter Margaret, whom they called "Peggy," was born premature, but in excellent health. She was the first new child to come into their cozy log home.

Next, we will do a little more setting up for the future. Getting another piece of the Dale family puzzle put in place.

# Chapter Six

## 1802: Liberty, Tennessee

Long before the move from Maryland—in fact since his youth—William Givan, the brother of long time family friend George Givan, had been quite sweet on Adam's young sister Sophia. She had always been friendly with him, but that was all it had ever amounted to. He didn't need just a female friend any more. Now he was determined to find his way into her heart.

William worked very hard, long hours to complete his house that spring. In fact he had started the previous fall and stopped work during the winter months. Only occasionally did he get any help from others and that only for tasks he felt he wasn't able to complete alone. But he had a method to his madness. When he had finally finished, it was time to win the prize.

"Come on, Sophia," he said one beautiful day in May 1802, "I have a home of my own now. You know I've cared about you since you were 12 and I was 16!"

Sophia smiled. She had always been a quiet one. However, since Will had never made any real effort at a true romance, she had only thought of him as a close buddy.

"It's been almost ten years. You're 21 now; I want to spend the rest of my life with you! We were meant to be together."

Sophia looked up into his amorous eyes and said, "Is that a proposal?"

"Well, I guess it is! And you're a grown woman now and you don't need your papa's permission anymore!"

"Yes."

"Yes, what?"

"Yes, I will marry you, Will Givan!"

The muscular Will grinned like a mule eating saw briars, grabbed Sophia by her wasp waist and slung her around like a small sack of flour! She was so shocked that she gasped for breath. He had never even tried to touch her before!

Theirs was the first wedding in the Dale family since their arrival in Tennessee. The family waited until Rev. Thomas Craighead, who came to Liberty once a month, was there the next time and he did the honors in Will's new home on 26 June.

Several other families had gotten clear titles to plots of land by this time and were building their homes as well. The Liberty community was really beginning to take shape now.

That same year, their darling daughter, Sarah, came into Adam and Polly's lives. They had no idea what a great pleasure she would come to be and to what phenomenal heights she would rise in life through her choice of a mate! We'll get to that a bit later in our story. She was freckle-faced, red-headed, had puffy cheeks and kept her family in stitches!

From the very beginning, Lizzie was jealous of the attention that Sarah was getting from their parents. Her resentment would only grow worse as they got older.

Adam's work of building a town, however, was barely getting started. In August he rode to Nashville and bought a Gunter's chain.

# Chapter Seven

## 1807: Liberty, Tennessee

"**W**ell, it's taken me almost five years, but I've finally gotten the town all laid out," Adam said one sunny day in May 1807. "Half acre cleared lots on the main road and streets going off of it that can be bought for a song! I just used 30 acres of my land."

Of course everyone for miles around knew what Adam was up to during his free time when he wasn't taking care of his crops and animals. It was obvious and the word got around fast. But his brothers had been so busy with proving up their own property and building their own houses that they hadn't taken time to assist him with the laying out of Liberty. After all, it was he, they reasoned, who would profit from the establishment of the town.

"Very good, Adam," John said. "Mama told me that you always knew how to organize things. Ever since you were just a youngun up North.

Back before I even was even a sparkle in Papa's eye."

Adam ignored John's apparent praises and continued to express his thoughts. Actually he didn't know but what they were left-handed compliments; just an effort to make excuses for not offering to help him get the lots cleared, surveyed and ready for sale. But he would find a way to get John, now 22 years old, involved. Adam knew his little brother better than he thought he did.

"I'm putting up for sale signs on them. We need businesses to come in."

"That we do! You're the man. I'll help you sell the lots," John offered.

Adam smiled. *Bingo!*

"Okay, I hope you really mean that! I'm putting you in charge of all of the lot sales. I've been told that our government is still having trouble regulating the value of foreign coins and since we have no established currency in our country yet, we will just have to play it by ear.

"Do what?"

"It's a metaphor I made up. You know, like somebody who can't read music and just picks out the notes on a guitar or banjo by the way a tune sounds."

"That's cute, big brother, but I don't think it'll ever catch on!"

"Probably not! Anyway, that doesn't amount to a hill of beans. What is important is the fact that I have decided that I'm only going to accept Spanish or Portuguese gold and silver coins. I'm fed up to here with England!" Adam said, making a quick cutting motion at his neck with his right hand. "Take offers and come to me for approval. I'll give you 10% of whatever we get out of each lot. Don't know how I'll manage to figure that, but we'll just have to ford that creek when we get to it."

Over the next year, finding buyers for the town lots was about as tough as pulling teeth with a string on a door knob. But some people back then were trying that too. Most of the residents there were dirt farmers. But they were getting a little attention from some of the folks they knew. Jared Walk, one of the Marylanders who had come in with the original settlers, who had worked in merchandise sales before moving to

Tennessee, bought the first lot and was already starting to build a general store on it.

Adam and John were trying to attract a blacksmith and a livery stable.

They knew that a real town was coming; it would just take a little time to develop.

# *Chapter Eight*

## 1809: Smith County, Tennessee

One warm June morning, Adam was as busy as a beaver working in his mill, greasing the cogs on the machinery, when he heard the door creak open.

*Another place I need to use this grease!* he said to himself.

Adam thought it might be John returning from New Orleans where he'd taken a large load of furs to trade for salt. He had gone on a keelboat on the Caney Fork, Cumberland and Mississippi Rivers. Lots of folks in Middle Tennessee had been doing it. Salt was going for a premium there in Liberty and John had set up a trading post on one of the town lots. It had been a little over four months, just about enough time for him to get back. Instead, though, he saw a hefty stranger sauntering up with a large Bible in one hand.

"Good morning, neighbor! Do you not need some corn ground?"

"No, Adam, my friend, my name is Cantrell Bethel. I'm a Primitive Baptist preacher," came his coarse, booming voice. "A lot of people have talked to me about you and I just had to come by and meet you."

Adam grinned.

"I hope some of it was good!"

"Oh, yes! It was all good! Everyone tells me what a fine man you are." Bethel's face was radiant and full of peace.

"Well, that's nice to hear!"

"Your brother Tom said that you are a faithful member of the Craighead's Presbyterian Church."

"Yes sir, they're good people. Brother Thomas Craighead comes here from Nashville the last Sunday of every month to teach his followers. We meet at my house. He's a little different from most Presbyterians in his teachings. And he's a really zealous man."

"I don't doubt that Brother Craighead is a very sincere fellow. I hear he's Irish."

"Yes—actually Scots Irish. He told me that some of his ancestors lived in Londonderry, the same as my papa. His family has long been in the Presbyterian ministry."

"That's really wonderful. I know that you have read the scriptures, Adam."

"Many times, dear Brother."

Would you please just look with me at Matthew 3:16?" Bethel said, thumping his right index finger on the open Bible in his other hand. "It says right here, 'As soon as Jesus was baptized, he went up out of the water.' Now, what do you reckon Jesus was doing in the Jordon River, pray tell, if he wasn't being immersed?"

Adam ducked his head and said nothing.

"Are we better than our Lord and Savior who told us to go about baptizing believers?"

Adam still didn't answer, so Bethel continued.

"I'm planning on starting a church here in Liberty. I'm having an organizational meeting this Wednesday night at my home. It's just to the west on the Nashville Road, up a little ways on the left. You can't miss it. There will be a lot of horses and buggies there. Won't you please come and join us?"

Adam tried hard but he couldn't think of a good excuse not to go, so he showed up that Wednesday night. He saw at once that a good many of his friends were also at the meeting and even his brother, William, who had arrived from Maryland with his wife, Nancy and young son, James, the year before.

"Listen to this man, Adam," William told him. "He has a head full of sense."

Adam nodded and turned his attention to the front of the room. Bethel was beginning to speak.

"What brought you to our area?" Adam asked Elder Bethel after the meeting."

"Well, I came here from Spartanburg County, South Carolina back in '02 to help my parents, Sampson Bethel and Mary Cantrell Bethel, organize the first church in this general area. It was up to the north of here near where they claimed land at Brush Creek that year. I've been serving as pastor up there since then. But God put the burden on me to plant new churches. This part of Tennessee is in bad need of churches."

Adam was impressed. Over the next few Sundays he met with the group for worship. Soon he decided to be immersed and he and his brother, William, became two of the 31 charter members of the new Salem Baptist Church. Adam was immediately elected as the church's first clerk. William, who played guitar, was appointed as the song leader.

The next time Craighead came to Liberty, Adam informed him that he had joined the Baptist Church and would no longer be hosting meetings. Craighead was understanding and gracefully bowed out.

For a while, the congregation met in the homes of some of the members. But they all wanted a permanent building.

Adam donated a large piece of land on the Nashville Road for the church and a cemetery. The little 25 X 30 foot log building, which quite a few of the male members worked diligently to build, was held together with mud stuffed with pieces of wood and stones. The corners were secured by wooden pegs. The floors and pews were made of split logs.

The church was lighted at night by grease lanterns and tallow candles. This was normal practice in that day and they were all just as happy as a dead pig in the sunshine to have a place to worship with a roof over their heads.

But no one could foresee what the Adam Dale family was to endure less than three years later.

# Chapter Nine

## January 1812: Liberty, Tennessee

Adam hadn't gotten up that night to stoke the fire and the cabin was colder than a well digger's destination. He was sleeping like a log with a pile of bed covers pulled over his tousled head the morning of 6 January 1812 when he was suddenly awakened by his frantic mother banging with both fists on his front door. Pulling his faded trousers over his new-fangled long johns, he drowsily made his way to the source of the knocking and threw up the large wooden latch.

"Adam! Adam! It's your papa! He's done gone and died on me!"

Adam stared blankly into his mother's desperate face. He was just plain numb! This couldn't be happening! *This had to be a nightmare.* He wanted to pinch himself. The family was still reeling from the shocking death of his brother, Tommy, at the young age of 32, from pneumonia the month before.

"What in God's name happened to Papa?" he heard his voice sing out as he pulled his mother in and pushed the door shut.

"When I woke up, your papa was still in bed. He's always up by 6:00, so I knew something must be bad wrong. I just went to wake him up to milk the cow. When I turned him over I saw that he wasn't breathing. I felt for a heartbeat, but he didn't have one!"

"Oh, Mama! I am so-o-o, so sorry!"

His sobbing mother laid her pale graying head over on his shoulder and wept uncontrollably. Adam could hold back his tears no longer.

"I think he just grieved himself to death over poor Tommy," his mother finally said, looking into Adam's gloomy face.

By this time, the rest of the family was streaming into the front room from the bedroom and down the ladder from the attic, joining in the mayhem. Each family member was asking what had happened, but they knew it was not good before they got an answer. They all united in hugs and sobs.

His cause of death was not determined, as there was no doctor around to examine him.

Elder Bethel was also heartbroken when the family asked him to speak at the funeral. He was a truly caring pastor and his eyes were teary as he brought the sad eulogy.

Thomas Dale, Sr. was laid to rest beside his namesake son behind Will and Sophie's house on the cold and rainy afternoon of Saturday, January 11th. He thus became the second person to be buried in what would become the Givan Cemetery.

Liberty and the surrounding area had been growing more rapidly each month. The news of the rich land was spreading and new settlers were coming into the area by the droves. Another large colony of families had come in from Maryland in 1808.

Roads had been cleared; cattle, hogs, goats, chickens and other poultry had been brought in.

Hunting hounds were common in the yards. In fact, Adam had gotten a Bluetick pup himself and named him Blue. The children spoiled him rotten and he got as lazy as a pig.

Jared Walk and his wife had opened their general store and were getting a whole heap of business. Several of Adam's lots had now been sold to aspiring businessmen. Adam's childhood friend, James Brattin, was also looking for a place to sell his farm produce that he'd been peddling door to door. Furs and crafts from Liberty were being traded all over the South and everyone was proud to be a part of this thriving colony. Adam was highly respected, even by the newer settlers, with whom he traded and who brought their corn to be ground at his mill. Adam's family was expanding and he had been able to amass a great deal of livestock and grain.

But that summer the cat would leave the house. And as the saying goes, "While the cat is away, the mice will play."

# Chapter Ten

## June 1812: Liberty, Tennessee

England had been constantly capturing American ships and their crews on the high seas and forcing them into the service of the king. Adam, being from the Maryland coast, not far from the large seaport of Baltimore, was madder than an old wet hen!

He was a patriot through and through. The U.S. Congress declared war on Britain and her Native allies on 17 June. The following day, Incumbent President James Madison signed the declaration into law.

With his late father's heroism in mind, Adam volunteered once more for military service and accepted a commission by the Tennessee militia of raising a large regiment of volunteers from Smith County to fight under General Andrew Jackson.

.

By then, Lizzie was growing into a comely young woman at age 16—well, she was closer to 17 by that time. And at least she thought she was a woman!

In addition to his original church at Brush Creek and the Salem Church, Elder Bethel, with the assistance of a man named Thomas Burgess, had established another new church on Sink Creek at a community known as Bildad, several miles to the east.

A handsome 20-year-old Baptist preacher named Samuel Gibbons from Madison County, Alabama had come to preach in his absence, so that the church, which had only been able to meet one Sunday a month of late, could have more regular services. Gibbons was ambitious, so he immediately announced that he would hold two services each Sunday that he preached, and even conduct Wednesday night Bible studies.

It had been rumored before his arrival that his family had money, so the pretty young Lizzie was excessively anxious to make his acquaintance.

That first Sunday morning, following the bene-diction, after most of the members of the congregation had shaken the young preacher's hand, Lizzie was anxiously waiting, flanked at her left by her apprehensive mother.

"Hey there, I'm Lizzie Dale! That was quite the sermon you preached this morning, Elder Gibbons!" Her voice was soft and her gaze was dead on and hypnotizing.

"Why thank you, young lady! Brother Bethel sure spoke awfully highly of your whole family!" Samuel nodded gracefully, as he flashed a broad smile, his perfect white teeth shining like little spikes of ivory. I hope you folks will be returning next Sunday. I expect that I'll be around for a good while filling in."

"What do you mean, 'next Sunday?' I'm looking mighty forward to coming back this very evening, Elder Gibbons! You can count on seeing me at each service, I'm sure!" Lizzie's dark auburn head was bobbing and a sly smirk lay on her shapely lips.

Samuel Gibbons glanced over at Polly and enthusiastically reached for her hand.

"You're to be congratulated, ma'am, for raising your daughter in the House of the Lord. It's a mite unusual for such a pretty young lass to be so motivated about church!"

If he had only known the true object of her zeal!

"My son Edward is also here with us. I think he's about your age." Polly pointed toward the door where the strapping young man was making a rapid exit. And this is my youngest, Sophie," she said, nodding at her fidgety seven-year-old spinning around in the aisle beside her. "Those three are mine, too: Tommy, Peggy and Sarah," she continued, her right index finger extended, "over there with their Aunt Martha."

Adam's 37-year-old sister, Martha Duncan, was motioning for them to hurry up and leave. She had been told in no uncertain terms by the young ones that they were hungry.

Her husband, Josiah, was taking their three children and heading for the door. But Lizzie wasn't anywhere near ready to go home yet.

"Elder Bethel told me that your husband is away in the service of our country," Gibbons said, looking at Polly.

"Yes, we're all very proud of him."

"Well, God bless him, God bless our country and God bless your fine family!"

Elizabeth never took her hungry eyes off of Samuel Gibbons' chiseled face and he was very keenly aware of it.

"Rock of ages, cleft for me! Let me hide myself in Thee! Let the water and the blood, From Thy riven side which flowed, Be of sin a double cure, cleanse me from its guilt and power!"

As the familiar closing hymn rang forth in the little log chapel, Lizzie stepped out of her hard log pew, made her way to the front and knelt gracefully.

Polly stood stark still, not knowing how to feel about her unpredictable daughter's apparent sudden desire for justification. If it were genuine she would be delighted. Somehow, though, her actions seemed a bit out of character. She could read her daughter like a book. Her face also told a different story.

"I believe Christ has chosen me as one of his own," she said softly.

"Praise God, Miss Lizzie!" Samuel said, joining her in thankful prayer.

As they rose, Samuel once again spoke aloud.

"When do you want to be baptized, Sister Lizzie?"

"Would next Sunday be too soon?"

"Hallelujah!" Samuel shouted, raising his right hand and waving it about.

"There is a fountain filled with blood, drawn from Immanuel's veins

"And sinners plunged beneath the flood; lose all their guilty stains

"Lose all their guilty stains; lose all their guilty stains

"And sinners plunged beneath the flood; lose all their guilty stains."

The enthusiastic members of the Salem Baptist congregation belted out the lyrics to the common baptismal hymn as Samuel plunged Lizzie under the muddy water of Smith Fork Creek.

"My sister, I baptize you in the name of the Father, the Son, and the Holy Ghost!"

"Praise the Lord!" the congregational response burst forth. Hands all around were lifted to the heavens as Lizzie shot up out of the gelid creek.

Every service found the entire Dale family in attendance. Polly saw to that. They were usually there before Samuel, even, thanks to Lizzie. Ole Blue would always follow them to church and wait patiently outside the door to follow them back home, even at night.

Since Cantrell Bethel was pastoring more than one church, Samuel preached a good deal of the time and became Elder Bethel's associate.

But Lizzie was suspiciously watching her first cousin, Elizabeth Duncan. They were close in age, and she was sure that she had seen her giving Samuel the look.

Lizzie would take no chances. She was already contriving her cunning moves.

# Chapter Eleven

## August 1812: Liberty, Tennessee

As time had marched on, Lizzie had devised clever ways to meet with Samuel when no one was close to them. With each tête-à-tête the two young people had shared a number of confidential experiences of their lives with one another and had become much more mutually endeared. But Polly was always surveilling them from a distance. She would never allow them to be truly alone. Lizzie was still only 16, and her strict mother would never let her forget it.

Polly had noticed right away that Lizzie was losing interest in her school work. She was putting too much effort into teaching her for her daughter not to do her dead level best. She thought that maybe she was being too stringent and it was having an adverse effect on Lizzie.

So, one Sunday that August, Polly invited Samuel to go home with them after church for dinner. He couldn't get enough of her fried chicken and apple pie! He was becoming addicted to this family and falling deeply in love with the tender young Lizzie.

Polly was now getting to really liking the youthful preacher and at least Lizzie wasn't running after a moonshiner's son.

Lizzie's birthday that year was on a Wednesday, so Polly again asked him to join them at their home for a celebration after a mid-week Bible study. Polly had baked a rich chocolate cake in a metal box in the fireplace for her seventeen year old, and brought it out of the pie safe that Adam had crafted after dinner that evening. Lighting the candles with thin strips of paper from the kitchen lamp, she smiled and looked over at Lizzie.

Lizzie closed her lovely eyes, made a wish and with one hefty puff blew out all of the candles.

"Why did you do that?" Samuel asked. "I've never seen candles on a cake before."

"Why, that's my birthday cake, silly!" Lizzie said with her signature giggle. "When a boy or girl has a birthday their mama puts the number of candles on it that they are years old. Then the birthday person makes a secret wish and blows them out! But you can't tell anybody your wish or it won't come true!"

"Oh, I see!" Samuel said, still amazed at this odd new tradition and slowly shaking his head.

Samuel saw this festive occasion as his perfect opportunity and knelt down on his right knee beside the long dinner table.

Polly simply assumed that he was about to pray a blessing for her daughter.

But instead, Samuel stared up into Lizzie's dark brown eyes and said in a most heartfelt tone: "Lizzie Evans Dale, would you do me the honor of becoming my wife?"

Lizzie jumped up and down like a puppy whose master had just returned from an extended trip.

"Yes! Yes! Of course I'll marry you! How did you know what I wished for?"

Polly was dumbfounded, raised her brows and shook her head. "I don't know what to say!"

Samuel looked over at her, his mouth agape and said apologetically, "Oh, I'm so sorry, ma'am! I should have asked you first. I just got excited! Can you please forgive me and give us your blessing?"

"Well, of course her father has to grant his approval, but you do have my blessing, Samuel." Polly smiled warmly.

Lizzie thanked her mother and gave her a big hug. Edward left the room and Sarah cried.

# Chapter Twelve

## November 1812: Liberty, Tennessee

"These two fine servants are my wedding gift to you, Sam. The young man is a bright and skillful blacksmith. His name is Joshua. You will be proud of what he is able to do. I even taught him to read."

Sam stared blankly at his brother, who had come from Alabama for his marriage ceremony, with a wrinkle forming in his forehead. He didn't know whether to thank him or tell him to take his "gift" back home with him.

"I'm not sure how I feel about this, David. I'm a preacher, you know!"

"I am well aware of that, my good brother, but they had servants in the Bible, you know." David cleared his throat. "Just treat them right and they'll be like your dear friends."

"And the girl?"

"Oh, her name is Sadie. She's 17 and will be good to help your wife around the house."

Sam glanced at Lizzie and she shrugged.

"Well, you can set up a shop for the blacksmith and he can earn us some extra money. Lord knows we sure can use it!"

In spite of the fact that Sam's parents were not paupers, they had not handed him everything on a silver platter. They had taught him to make his own way.

"Okay, David. Thank you for caring about me," Sam said, relaxing his mood a little.

Sam's sister, Honor, who had come for the wedding from Centerville, Tennessee, gave both of her brothers a frown and started talking to her husband.

Sam vowed to treat Joshua and Sadie kindly, never think of them as slaves, but wards, and reward them for their loyalty and hard work.

John told Sam to use one of the town lots on which to build a shop for Joshua. He felt certain that Adam would be in agreement with the lot being a wedding gift. Now that problem had been solved. As well as the one for a town blacksmith!

Adam, of course, had been away at war and unable to attend the wedding, but when he had gotten word of the betrothal from Polly in a letter, he was incredibly pleased with her choice in a husband and had given his hearty approval. He trusted his wife's appraisal of Samuel. Perhaps getting married young was alright, he reasoned, if she had selected a proper mate. Sam was everything that a young girl's father could have asked for in that day and time.

The simple ceremony was held at Salem Church on 19 November 1812 and happily performed by the cheerful Elder Bethel.

Samuel had been allowed to stay in a small cabin beside the Bethel home, where they were headed after the ceremony. David had kept the servants until the following day.

Edward had scribbled the words "just married" on the back of Adam's carriage which he had loaned them for the occasion.

Some of the rice which was thrown at the couple as they dashed out from the church to the carriage went down the front of Lizzie's blouse and she cursed so softly that Sam couldn't hear her.

# Chapter Thirteen

## 1813: Liberty, Tennessee

One day the next fall while John Dale was busily toiling at the mill, putting up sacks of meal on a shelf for sale, the door flung open and a pudgy middle-aged man came in whom he had never seen before in his life.

"Howdy neighbor! I need a bushel o' corn ground. I bought it from one o' your neighbors, William Boyd."

"Okey dokey! We'll get 'er done for you. Just a peck toll out of each bushel. I don't believe I know you, mister. Do you live around here somewhere?"

"Not too awful far from here! I bought me a nice parcel o' land over yonder to the east a few miles," he said, pointing in the general direction of his property. "It's a great big ole hill. I got me 75 acres and built me a nice little log house at the bottom o' that there hill."

John smiled and nodded, thinking hard about what his customer had told him.

"Oh, by the way, my name's Joseph Snow, my friends just call me Joe," he said, reaching out for a handshake. "I came down here last spring from Delaware!"

"Yeah? Delaware? We're from Maryland, I guess you may know!"

"Yes, sir! So I heard. I learned about your nice little town here from some o' your sister-in-law's folks up near where I lived in Delaware! That's why I moved to this area. I'm a-gonna call my place 'Snow Hill!' Your town in Maryland was named for some o' my relatives!"

"Is that so? Small world, ain't it?" John's eyebrows were raised. "Hey, why didn't you just stake a claim to some land instead of buying it? There's still plenty to be had not far from here, you know."

They were both having to raise their voices to be able to hear one another over the din of the mill.

"Well, I guess that's a pretty darn good question, young man, and I'm a-gonna answer it for ya! The place I bought was already staked out and had a bunch o' cleared land and a nice spot for a house right in the big bend in the road. Saved me a whole heap o' work! And I got it for next to nothing."

"Makes sense," John said in a lower voice now, as he handed Joe Snow his large cotton sack of corn meal.

"Hey, did you know that a young fellow named Jesse Allen is buildin' a gristmill over on Eagle Creek? He's gonna be able to grind both corn and wheat."

"Naw, I hadn't heard anything about it. But I know ole Jesse. He came here not long after we did from Maryland. Good to hear. I knew that he'd built him a little cabin over that way somewhere."

"Some folks are already startin' to grow a little wheat, you know."

"Now, that I *had* been told. I believe there's a nice field of it next to Eagle Creek, come to think of it."

"I've also heard that someone else over in Jesse's neck o' the woods is bringing in a cotton gin and a distillery! You can help spread the word."

"Oh, my! My big brother, Adam will be quite impressed. Too bad you can't meet him. He's the one that started this town, you know. He's away fighting the Creek Indians."

"Yeah, I heard that, too," Joe answered in a mumbled tone.

About that time, the door swung open again and Sam and Lizzie walked in.

"This is my niece, Lizzie, and her husband, Sam Gibbons," John said.

"Hey there, mister!" Lizzie playfully slurred her words and giggled.

*Uh, oh! Now here's trouble!* Joe thought, but only said, "Good to meet you folks," tipped his hat and hurriedly left.

# *Chapter Fourteen*

## 1814: Liberty, Tennessee

**"I**'m sure proud that we stayed here, Lizzie!" Sam said the next New Year's Day.

The hard Jack Frost glistened on the window pane as the bright morning sun snuck between the crests of the hills from the east. At least most people in Liberty had now been able to get glass windows!

"Yeah, me too," Lizzie dittoed; as she thought just the opposite, wondering what magic realms lay beyond this rural wilderness.

Samuel had continued to live in Liberty, mostly because he had married Lizzie, and it had turned out to be a boon for him. His little wife was still very young and not yet ready to cut the apron strings that bound her to her mother.

Sam had laid claim to a fifty acre slice of the wonderful Middle Tennessee land that was drawing so many outsiders to the area. Word had spread quickly about the rich soil, beautiful landscapes, wild game and abundant streams of clear, cold water.

Sam didn't want any more land than fifty acres, though Liz didn't understand why. She would have taken a thousand if she could have gotten it. But it was all that Sam felt he could care for; he had told her so.

Having Joshua had already begun to pay off for Sam by the dawn of 1814.

Adam hadn't been present to object, of course, but Polly had written him about the slaves and he wasn't too crazy about the idea of his son-in-law owning people.

"It's just not right," he wrote back to her.

One thing Polly always did was be honest with her husband; both about things which she perceived as good and the unpleasant ones.

With a lot of help from Joshua and what he could beg from his brother-in-law, Edward, when he wasn't too busy, Sam had built a nice log house for them, a small two room cabin for the servants to sleep in and a nice little shop for Joshua. He was following the example of his neighbors in laying off and planting crops on the little farm.

Lizzie had put Sadie in charge of cooking, making lye soap, washing their clothes in the creek, hanging them out on clothes lines tied between trees and carrying in firewood. In the winter the clothes had to be brought inside to keep them from freezing solid on the lines. Sam had tied a rope across in front of the fireplace. Lizzie didn't like the appearance of it, but she didn't know any other option, so she just had to grin and bear it.

Sam had set up the shop for Joshua with tools that he had ordered from Mr. Walk at the store and he was now being kept busy shoeing everyone's horses around Liberty. Sometimes he even stayed there at night when he worked late. This, naturally, had given Sam a considerable amount of extra income. Some of it was paid for in chickens, guineas and pigs—and that was all well and good. Shoot, he'd even been given a young heifer to raise to be a milk cow.

A fine-looking livery stable had been opened on the lot on the right side of the blacksmith shop by another enterprising young investor who was the son of one of the later Maryland immigrants.

Lizzie had nothing but disdain for all blacks, but for Sam's sake and because Joshua was adding to their income, she tried to bite her tongue and be somewhat tolerant of them. Then the work that Sadie was doing took those chores off of her. That wasn't all bad. She was enjoying having so much free time, though she really wanted to have some rich friends.

On 9 August the Creek War ended when Red Stick leader William Weatherford surrendered to Andrew Jackson. The Treaty of Fort Jackson had been signed near Wetumka, Alabama.

Everyone in Liberty welcomed Adam back home with a big party! Polly was overjoyed!

Before long things were getting pretty much back to normal. Adam added to his stories all of the experiences that he had while away, and the family listened; all but Liz, who lived in her own little world of self desire, and wasn't living in her parents' home anymore.

Close to the end of the year, Adam's brother, William, felt a call to the ministry and was ordained by Elder Bethel for going out to help him establish other churches. Other members of the Bethel family were getting involved, too. Another church member, John Fite was also being prepared for ministry.

Speaking of the Fites, Lizzie's Aunt Martha told her that fall that her daughter, Elizabeth, had gone with John Fite's brother, Leonard, to his hometown in North Carolina and married him! *Whoopie!* Even though she and Sam had been married for two years, she still had never forgotten that her cousin had been attracted to him!

Yes, Sam's ministerial position had been morphing, so to speak. But something else unexpected was also on the horizon. Something that would lead to an entirely different life for Adam and his family.

# Chapter Fifteen

## 1815: Liberty, Tennessee

**E**d couldn't help but stare. He thought that he had never seen any woman so beautiful in his whole life! And he was soon to discover that she was also smart and witty! His sisters were lovely, but they were his sisters, for heaven's sake! They didn't count.

It was January 1815. Her name was Anne Lewis Moore. She was the daughter of Rev. Nathanial Moore, a former Methodist circuit rider preacher from Columbia, Tennessee who was now an evangelist. He had come to Liberty to run a revival, as he had done in a number of other communities in Middle Tennessee. Moore had set up a brush harbor with the permission of the owner of the land he was using, a Johnny come lately who was a Methodist, and was drawing crowds from all over the region, thanks to the best type of advertising, word of mouth.

Moore's preaching was powerful, arising from the spiritual revival of the early 1800s. Elder

Bethel, regardless of the difference of belief, rather than discourage the effort, invited him to use the Salem Church building so that the attendees could have heat and light for the night services. The meetings went on every evening for most of a month.

Moore's tone of voice was actually a lot like that of Elder Bethel, who was noted for his thunderous delivery; but a new face always grabs attention. Sort of like the saying about a new broom sweeping clean.

Bethel knew that Moore wouldn't be there forever and reasoned that he would reap the rewards in the long run by taking in the new converts which he believed were actually chosen and making sure that they were "properly baptized."

The physical and spiritual attraction between Edward and Anne was undeniable. Within a week after the revival began they had started sitting together at the services and spending a lot of time talking before and after church.

When the revival ended and the Moore family left, Ed bought a fast gaited Appaloosa gelding from a family friend and kept the roads hot between Liberty and Columbia. He had to go through Nashville, though it was not a direct route, because of the roads. It was a hard three to four day ride each way, but it was all pleasure for Ed. You know what they say about love being blind.

Edward was already 28 years of age and Polly knew that theirs was a wonderful match. Ed wasn't getting much work done around home anyway. And Polly knew that he wasn't getting any younger, either.

"Why don't you just go ahead and marry that nice girl?" she asked, after he had returned from a visit in late March.

Ed thought for sure that he could see a colorful bird of paradise growing in their front yard and that a choir of heavenly angels had gathered all around it. He was just plumb certain that he could hear their joyful singing echoing through the rolling hills.

Ed hastened his return to Columbia and asked the Reverend Moore for his daughter's hand in marriage.

The entire Moore family was as pleased as punch, and all of the Dale clan traveled to

Columbia in a covered wagon caravan for their happy wedding on 22 May.

No one suspected that this union would eventually change the course of Dale family history forever.

But right now we must fast forward five years to find out about another major calamity.

# Chapter Sixteen

## 1820: Liberty, Tennessee

"**H**ave you seen your brother this morning?" Polly asked Liz after walking down the hill to her house.

It was mid-October and the cool autumn day was just getting underway.

"No, Mama! Didn't he go out and milk Jers this morning?"

"Nope, your papa went to the barn and milked when he saw that the bucket was still setting in the house empty. He's out looking for Thomas right now."

"Thomas! Thomas!" Liz could hear her father's voice in the far distance echoing through the ravines, and headed toward it. But Peggy, who still lived with her parents, had gotten a head start on her and caught up to him first. Old Blue was close at her heels.

"Where have you looked, Papa?" Peggy had asked when she joined him in the yard.

"All around here. But I noticed that my gun is missing from the rack over the fireplace. He must be out hunting. We need to head up to the mill and look around there," Adam said. "He always goes up that way when he's out hunting." Blue stuck his nose in the air and let out a melancholy howl. Then he turned and gazed up sadly into Adam's worried eyes.

"Now why aren't you with him, you lazy hound?" he said. What he didn't know was that their faithful companion had been with Thomas when he left that morning.

Blue led the way, and when they all reached the mill, Thomas was nowhere to be seen. Adam noted, however, that the wheel was not turning freely, so he walked around to the back of it. Thomas' limp body was lying face down in the cold creek against the bouncing mill wheel.

Adam's eyes filled up tears. He bent over, lifted his son gently in his arms and cried out at the top of his lungs. Blue just looked up pitifully and joined him in a gloomy duet.

Peggy screamed. Liz arrived and started crying.

The following year after Ed and Anne were wed things just hadn't been the same in Liberty for the Dale family.

Liz was gloomy for a while. But 22-year-old Thomas, the only brother that had been left at home, missed Ed so badly that he didn't care about much of anything around home anymore. The education he had been given by his mother and the knowledge his father had passed on to him of the work which had to be done had prepared him for his basic duties on the farm and helping out at the mill. But he had wanted a lot more out of life that just wasn't happening. He daydreamed of living in a city and what he could learn there. He had thought a lot about joining his brother in Columbia; but he had felt obligated to help around home, since Adam had no other sons to take over for him in the long haul.

Very early that morning he had decided to take his father's musket and go deer hunting, intending to milk the cow when he returned. He had tossed and turned that night, sleeping very little.

The leaves on the sourwoods along Smith Fork Creek just past the mill were a brilliant crimson and he was gazing up at them as he meandered north along the cliff's crooked edge at the brink of the creek in the darkness.

A large speckled brown owl had hooted and flown down directly toward him. Ducking to miss the huge bird, Thomas had lost his footing and tumbled head-over-heels down over the cliff into the rushing creek, his head striking a sharp rock.

Thomas' funeral was the saddest of occasions. Ed wrote his parents saying that he was not able to come home afterward. In reality, he had just decided that he couldn't deal with the knowledge that Thomas was no longer there. Adam, also, wasn't himself after that for a very long time.

To try to get his mind off of the loss of his son, Adam subtly approached his friend, Daniel Alexander, one of the newer Maryland settlers, almost two weeks later, about rumors that he'd been hearing.

"Dan, you've been a big help around here, and a lot of encouragement to me with getting the town started. I also appreciate all you've done for my family and helping me get in my corn earlier this fall. But your property is a good ways from here. There's a great deal of opportunity up there to the northwest close to Brush Creek where your land lies. More people are coming in up that way all the time, I've been told."

"You must have been reading my mind, Adam. I have already decided to start a new community; in fact, a new town," he nodded, "like you did, on the other end of my place. You were my inspiration. I'm gonna call it Alexandria."

Adam was truly happy for his good friend.

Alexandria would also become a thriving little town and the Snow Hill community would grow somewhat as well, welcoming new migrants.

But after things seemed to be getting some better for the Dale family, a few years later, the death angel would sweep in again—with a vengeance.

# Chapter Seventeen

## February 1829: Columbia, Tennessee

Ed's children clung tightly to his pant legs. His large silvery tears went forth like a gushing river as he turned his head away from the wooden casket being lowered into the cold, hard ground by long leather straps. As Lizzie pressed in upon him, he hugged her neck tightly and whispered, "Let's go, Sis! I can't take anymore."

Lizzie pushed her arm lovingly around his waist and pulled him slowly away, in the direction of the waiting carriage. Ed and Anne's other family members, on both sides, felt thoroughly helpless. The strongest bond that any of the Dale siblings had was definitely the one between Lizzie and Ed.

Ed's mind was in a mad whirl. As he walked gradually away from his wife's final resting place, he could hear and sense the finality of the soil being shoveled into the dark foreboding hole.

He was harshly reliving those final moments with his precious Anne when his trembling hands had grasped hers and he had stared weepy-eyed into her pale fleeting features.

"You can't leave me, my sweet love. You're everything to me and our children!"

Anne had whispered her answer ever so faintly.

"I will always be with you, Darling. Care for our dear children. They will need you more than ever now. I will be resting with our dear Lord. I will see you again some sweet day."

Anne's lovely orbs had seemed to freeze in a glaring openness and her faint breath had come no more.

Ed's head had fallen to her stiffened breast and his tears had come in torrents from his swollen, reddened eyes.

Ed had moved to Columbia and joined the Methodist Church ten years earlier when he and Anne had said their joyful 'I dos.' His father-in-law had gotten him a job as a bookkeeper there at the church right off the bat. The couple had been very happy and now had four lovely children: Elvira, Mary, Anne, and their only boy, young Nathaniel.

It had been nine years and Ed still refused to talk to anyone about Thomas' death.

In January 1829, Adam and Polly, along with Adam's mother, Elizabeth, had been visiting Ed and his family in Columbia when the 82-year-old Elizabeth Dale had taken a dire case of pneumonia and soon passed away. Ed had again gone totally off his feed and was still out of commission.

But now, this! He just could endure nothing more.

Anne, who had been caring for ailing Granny Dale, had contracted the dreaded disease herself and had died less than a month later on 13 February. Both women had now been buried at Greenwood Cemetery there in Columbia.

Ed was now obviously even more completely and irrevocably devastated. As if Thomas' and his mother's deaths hadn't been enough to practically kill him.

With both his mother and his wife, he had been right smack dab in the middle of the horror that was going on. He couldn't just pretend that it hadn't happened, like he had with Thomas. His children were so distraught that no one could begin to soothe them. Ed needed to be both father and mother to his children, but he didn't think he was made of that strong a bolt of cloth.

Anne's parents asked Ed if they could keep the children until he had a little time to get himself calmed down. It also allowed them to have a part of their daughter to hold on to for a little while longer.

But the year was barely getting started. Another colossal alteration was coming in 1829 which no one could foresee except the conniving little Liz.

# *Chapter Eighteen*

## March 1829: Centerville, Tennessee

Liz and Sam, to those living around them, had seemingly enjoyed a pleasant marriage for over 17 years. But Sam, though still active in the church, had almost quit preaching. Since Liz's Uncle William and others were now helping Elder Bethel with preaching at Salem and starting new churches, Samuel was staying busy doing other things. He was spending most of his time building up their little farm and accumulating money and livestock to secure their future. He had also been filling in occasionally for Adam at the mill.

The years had been gentle to Liz and her beauty had seemed only to intensify as she matured.

Lizzie just smiled and looked pretty. She had received furtive looks from quite a few other men, both at church and in town, which secretly pleased her to no end.

But no children had been born to their union and Liz wondered if she would always be barren. She envied Ed for having such fine offspring.

The church had been fortunate to have Samuel to work with the youth and continue to preach on occasion; but Elizabeth noticeably had shown no genuine spiritual fervor. She was blasé, to say the least. Life for the couple had begun to grow stale and lonely.

It was 4:00 o'clock on a cool Saturday afternoon. The days were beginning to get longer and it was still bright daylight. John Phillips heard horse's hooves beating against his hard driveway just out of Centerville, Tennessee. Then he heard a horse's loud neigh and a familiar voice shouting "Whoa!"

Looking out the window, he recognized his brother-in-law, Samuel, stepping down from a buggy helping his sister-in-law, Elizabeth and another man whom he didn't know. He hollered for Sam's sister and out they both ran to greet their visitors.

Liz had asked Sam to spend some time with Ed in Columbia after Anne's funeral to show support and try in whatever small way possible to comfort him.

"Lizzie, dear, while we are down here this close I would like to go see my sister, Honor, over in Centerville. Ed can go with us," Sam had said one day.

"What do you think, Ed?" Liz had asked.

Ed hadn't answered.

"It'll do you good to get away, Ed," Sam had told him.

The dirt roads were still not in great shape, but after Ed had finally agreed, they had hitched their horse to their buggy and headed to the northwest. It was a long, tiresome trip, but they had gotten there near the end of the third day, camping along the road at night.

On the way, however, Ed had realized that the trip really would be good for him; he had already started feeling some better emotionally by the first night. He had just needed some sibling prodding.

Honor was really thrilled to see her brother. She just hated living so far away from him and never getting to visit. They hadn't seen Sam and Lizzie but once since their wedding, and that was when they had visited them in Liberty several years ago.

"I want to start a mercantile here in town, but I need a partner. At least someone to help me get the store set up," John told his guests that first night at dinner. "I just don't know anyone here in Centerville who has the means and the desire to give me a hand."

"I know someone who might just fill the bill!" Ed said with a gleam in his eye.

"Are *you* interested?" John said eagerly, his eyes growing sharp.

Ed was smiling and nodding.

"Would you like to go see the building I have picked out? The owner died a couple of weeks ago and his children have put it up for rent." John was also nodding, as if attempting to use his persuasive powers in case Ed had any doubts. "It's in an excellent location, right on Central Avenue! We wouldn't need but about $300 to get started. I already have $150 if you can come up with the rest."

"Sure," Ed said, "let's go look it over in the morning! I have the other $150. That's no problem. My life has been horrible since Anne left me. I need to get my mind on something else and I'm already a bookkeeper. I can help you get the business started and be a silent partner. Of course I have to get back to Columbia before long to care for my children."

That night, after Honor had expressed her feelings to him about never getting to see one another, Sam enthusiastically approached Liz with a proposition of his own.

"Isn't this great? You and I could move down here to Centerville and be close to my sister. You could help look after Ed's business interests. And we both miss Ed. Remember how he and I used to go fishing together back in Liberty? We would be closer to him, too. I wouldn't have any difficulty selling our little farm and the blacksmith shop. Why, I had a man ask me about the shop just a few days ago. He told me that his son wants to take up the trade."

Liz was silent for a moment, but she was truly tickled to death. Now she could get what she really wanted and Sam would think he was the cause of it!

"I'd be willing to move to Columbia," she said, "if you had a job there!"

"That's fair enough." Sam rubbed the stubble of beard that he had started to cultivate on his chin, thinking that her suggestion was a reasonable compromise. "I'm sure Ed could help me. He's been living there for several years and knows a lot of people in Columbia.

Ed and John struck up a partnership deal that next morning and shook hands on it. Ed was also overjoyed that Liz and Sam were seriously talking about moving to Columbia.

"It's like a load is lifted off of me! I promise I will get you a good job," he told Sam. "I know a storekeeper who is looking for a clerk. I'll give you a great reference!"

So Ed stayed in Centerville to help John while Liz and Sam went back home to Liberty to plead their case with Adam.

# Chapter Nineteen

## Summer 1829: Columbia, Tennessee

"**W**elcome to Columbia, Papa!" Ed exclaimed enthusiastically, as he reached up and helped his father down from his carriage.

When Liz had told Adam of their plans to move to Columbia, he had been sorely perplexed. He had made a good home all these years with friends and family in Liberty. He had founded the town, for goodness sake! And he owned a large farm and a thriving business. He had also taken over some of his father's land. He would really miss that mill if he moved!

But he knew that he must consider the big picture. Their young son, Thomas, was dead and Edward had been in Columbia for several years. Now Liz would be moving there as well. His grandchildren were also in that city and his precious mama was buried there.

So when Sam had sold his farm and the shop, Adam had let his brothers and sisters buy his property and let John take over the mill.

Adam really hated to leave his sister Sophia behind. Her husband, Will Givan, had died on 3 November 1822. But she still owned the home with the family cemetery in the back where their father and brother, Tommy, as well as Will, were buried.

Old Blue was now 17 and Adam had asked Sophia and her children to keep him there, which they were glad to do. That hound dog was like family to them as well, and they knew he was too old to move so far.

However, Adam's sister, Martha, who had also lost her husband, Josiah Duncan, just two years earlier, had always been close to Adam and Polly and had decided to move with them.

Soon after the move, Adam purchased a pretty white board house close to town and joined Miller's Baptist Church, where he agreed to serve as an Elder. Here, Elders were more like overseers or deacons. The church was thrilled!

Sam had bought a house in town, painted a pale blue. The move to the little city had put Sam and Lizzie into a higher society environment and Elizabeth quickly became restless. Here, something else was also different.

Liz gazed out her large front window, straining her inquisitive ears. She could barely perceive the conversation on the street in front of their home. One of their single neighbor ladies seemed quite smitten by her handsome, now fully-bearded, husband and always made certain to be out in the yard where she could strike up a conversation with him each day when he came in from work.

"Good evening, Sam! Isn't it a lovely day today?" she said in an alluring tone. "Did you have a good day at work?"

"Yes, Daisy! A very nice day, indeed! Can't complain. I enjoy my work, and it meets the need. God is good!"

"Remember, I'm here if you ever need to talk!"

"Yes, ma'am. Have a nice evening!"

This annoyed Liz greatly, but she didn't mention it to Sam because he had not seemed to be responsive to her attempts at friendship. She really didn't start to worry a lot until another noisy lady in the neighborhood told Liz that she had seen the woman with Sam at the store where he worked and they had seemed awfully chummy with one another. Then Liz became insanely jealous and swore that Samuel had cheated on her.

"Now you know better than that! You know good and well that you're my only love, Lizzie, darling!"

"Well, I sure had better be!" she snapped.

But Liz let her jealousy fester inside her like an ulcer, sucking the very life out of her. She made up her mind that she would find a way to deal with him!

Edward was feeling considerably better than he had been immediately after Anne's death, but he still felt terribly lost and forlorn. He had never been a loner. When he was young, there had always been Lizzie to stay close to. Then he had Anne. He knew that his unhappy children needed a permanent mother figure in their lives.

At church he became acquainted with a charming widow named Frances Baird who was the mother of three bright children: Mary, Paul and Eliza Ann.

They began spending a good amount of time together; occasionally going out to eateries and visiting in one another's homes. Finally, Ed was beginning to feel a tiny ray of hope entering his dreary life.

The fact that Frances was two years older than Ed made no difference to either of them. After courting for a few months, they both decided that they truly needed one another and their children were getting along famously. The couple was united in wedlock there at the church that year on 22 September.

Their marriage was definitely a good thing for all of them.

But in regard to another matter, it wouldn't be long until Adam would hit the roof!

# Chapter Twenty

## 1830: Columbia, Tennessee

In late May 1830, while Liz was visiting in her parents' home, Adam pulled an article out of one of his desk drawers which he had torn from the *Columbia Herald* just a few days earlier.

"I'm so dad-blamed upset with Andy Jackson that I could spit nails!" he screamed. "I voted for him for President because I served under him all that time and we had a really good relationship! But now he's gone and signed that consarned Indian Removal Act into law! I knew that Congress had voted for it, but I really thought that he would refuse to sign it! Do you see that?" Adam was shoving the article into Liz's face. "I fought with him in the Creek War because I wanted us to have a lasting peace with the Indians, not to remove all of them out West and put them on reservations! The treaty gave the government enough of their land!"

Liz just turned her head and stared out the window.

"Why do you even care one lick about those wild savages?" Liz turned toward her father and growled like a bear, making clawing motions with her hands in the air.

"Wild savages? What the devil are you talking about, Liz? The Indians are human beings with feelings just like we have! And they were in this land long before we were! I swanny, gal, I don't think you care one bit about anybody but your own dang self!"

Elizabeth just shook her head and walked away.

**N**ine months, to the day, after Ed and Frances' wedding; on 22 June, Edward Washington Dale II was born and Ed once again seemed more like his old self.

"Now I have a son with my own name to carry it forward after I am no longer here!" he told Frances excitedly.

They both smiled and pulled one another close in a long, meaningful embrace.

Ed was content now, at least for a good while; but Liz was far from it! The evil green dragon of jealousy had completely overwhelmed her. Her cycle of hate and reign of terror were set to begin their race with destiny.

# Chapter Twenty-one

## 1830: Centerville, Tennessee

In early July, Samuel asked Liz to go with him back to Centerville to visit with John and Honor again.

Liz pursed her mouth in a malicious smile. "Sure!" she said, "Why not?"

*This is wonderful*, her vile thoughts rushed in. *We'll be a long way from my parents! I can take care of my problem with Sam once and for all!*

They arrived in Centerville on Tuesday, July 13th and spent the night. The next morning, Liz arose early and prepared breakfast before Honor had a chance to do so. Luckily for her, her hostess seemed greatly pleased when she came in and saw what a fine favor that Liz had done for her. But she hadn't seen the small container she had taken from her purse when she had prepared Sam's plate.

Up in the middle of the day, Liz was casually talking girl stuff with Honor in the kitchen where she was prolifically cooking ham and sweet potatoes for their dinner. John was occupying his time entertaining Sam in the sitting room.

"I'm not feeling too pert—matter of fact, I feel terribly peculiar. My stomach is cramping something awful!" Sam said, as he sat down rapidly on the paisley divan. "Would you please fetch me a drink of water?"

About that time, Sam's head plunged forward and green guile flew all over the polished floor.

"Gadzooks, man!" John started; then glanced down at the horrid sight. "Of course I will!"

John rushed into the dining area, grabbed the tin dipper lying next to the porcelain wash pan and dipped it full out of the wooden water bucket.

By the time he had gotten it back into the parlor, Sam had fallen limply to the hardwood floor, face first, landing directly in his own appalling vomit.

"Liz, Honor! Hurry!" he yelled, "Sam's awful bad off! I'm going to get Doc Sebastian!

Holding her nose with her left hand and gagging, Honor worked quickly to get her brother cleaned up. It seemed to her that the doctor would never get there.

By the time John had finally arrived with Dr. Sebastian, Sam was unconscious. The diagnosis came right away.

"This is highly unusual. He has yellow fever and black tongue. See? His features are badly distorted, and his visage is sinister! What on earth has he eaten?"

"We haven't had our dinner yet! Oh, well, he did eat some eggs and bacon a few hours ago for breakfast and had some biscuits and coffee. But his own dear wife fixed that, herself!"

The concerned doctor slowly shook his head and frowned.

"Well could he have drunk some bad whisky last night?"

Under any other circumstances this might have seemed humorous to these women. But not now, certainly not now!

"Sam is a Hard Shell Baptist preacher and a tee-totaller. He doesn't drink at all!" Honor strained to answer.

Liz just sat there blank-faced.

The concerned physician paced the floor and stayed with them for the duration. Before long, the sun had set and the last-quarter moon was slowly rising. Dark clouds hung low and blackness was engulfing the house.

Honor lit the lamp in the parlor next to the divan. They all heard a sharp gasp. Samuel had expired.

The meal which Honor had prepared had long grown cold, but no one was hungry except Elizabeth and she durst not let it be known.

Samuel had been exceptionally wise as a young man and had gotten a will prepared before his 24th birthday, in 1816. He had named his brothers-in-law, John Phillips and Robert W. Roberts, executors. He had willed Honor $100, and a shotgun to her son. His entire estate and two slaves went to Elizabeth. That was a huge mistake!

After the funeral at the little Primitive Baptist Church that the Phillips' attended and burial in the cemetery there, Liz returned home alone.

She did her best to appear to be in bereavement, always wearing black clothing in public. But she couldn't grieve forever, now could she?

# *Chapter Twenty-two*

## 1831: Huntsville, Alabama

Fresh foliage was shooting forth from the trees and the new grass was coming up a lovely shade of jade green the next morning as they entered the small quiet North Alabama city.

This adventure had begun two days earlier in Columbia.

"Would you care to ride with me to Huntsville to buy a new carriage, Ed?" Adam had said.

"Why certainly, Papa! When do you want to go?"

"Tomorrow."

"Take me with you, too!" Lizzie had peeped up.

Spring had finally sprung and Adam had felt the need for a new carriage, as his old one was showing a great deal of wear and tear. It would also need new wheels before long. He had learned from a close friend at church that there was a factory in Huntsville which manufactured high-quality carriages, buggies and surreys.

Adam and Ed had already been in the carriage the next morning waiting for Liz. As she had been heading out the door, she had looked over at her mother.

"Keep my buck and my wench busy while I'm gone. Don't let them have it too easy!"

"Why I'd be ashamed of myself, Elizabeth!"

Liz had just scowled and slammed the door behind her. Polly was flabbergasted. Sometimes she didn't know what to think or do anymore. Liz was a grown woman and she couldn't treat her like a spoiled child, but sometimes her actions made her seem for the world like one.

The trip down into Alabama had been exceptionally pleasant. Strong March winds had given way to warm spring breezes which had pursued them and the tranquil April sun had brightened their way.

They had camped that first night next to a wide, beautiful gurgling stream called Richland Creek just south of the newly formed little town of Cornersville. As they were setting around the campfire they had heard the distant cry of a mournful whip-poorwill. Adam loved it. This reminded him of his trek to Liberty from

Maryland—but this time he had his two older children along! Always positive, he had taught himself to forget the bad experiences quickly.

The rhythmic motion of the water on the creek rocks that night was conducive to peaceful sleep and Adam had sweet dreams of his beloved Polly and a good future. Dreams which would soon be shattered.

One more night had been spent camping near the limits to the city of Huntsville because darkness had overtaken them.

As Adam pulled into the carriage factory, he saw that there was a lovely white picket fence around the factory and the house next door. He then noticed a most attractive small wisteria tree blooming in front of it. The scent of the blossoms tingled his sensitive sinuses, but he didn't allow such a small distraction to bother him in the least. He was merely soaking in this superb time with his older children.

Suddenly plain, crisp words rang out as a sharply dressed, tall figure of a man emerged from the big building.

"Hello, may I help you?"

"Yes, I'm looking to purchase a new carriage," Adam said in a happy, friendly manner.

"Well, sir, you came to the right place!"

The clear voice was that of the factory owner, Philip Flanagan.

While Adam and Ed were making their rounds of the grounds, trying to decide on which style carriage would best suit Adam's needs, Lizzie was busily putting on the Ritz, introducing herself to Flanagan.

"Hello there, I'm Lizzie! You have a nice place here, Mr. Flanagan! How long have you been in business?"

"Three years, but I've been building carriages for a good while longer. I studied the craft under a young fellow named Rice down in Tuscaloosa. He's still in business there, in a partnership with another man."

"Are you married?"

"Not exactly. But I used to be. I'm a widower."

"You must get lonely at times. I'm a widow, myself. I know what it can be like being alone." Liz was displaying her saddest countenance.

*Perhaps he's more in my social class*, she thought, *he certainly dresses and acts like a man of great wealth.*

"Yes, ma'am," she heard him say. "I married young. My children are grown and out on their own now. I do get a bit lonesome sometimes. I just haven't met anyone that I care about enough to marry yet." Flanagan was looking her over and liked what he saw.

Adam was calling him and his voice seemed to be far away, as in a tunnel. Flanagan had to drag himself away from all of this wonderful attention just to make a sale.

"I'll take this one!"

"Good choice. I sell a lot of those. People seem to like the new wheel design. You see the price marked in chalk there on the side."

"Yes, I do. That is satisfactory. Here is your money! Would you kindly dispose of my old carriage, Mr. Flanagan? I have no need for it now and we don't have another horse to pull it back to our home in Columbia, Tennessee."

"I will be more than happy to, Mr. Dale. I'm sure there will be some reusable parts on it."

As they were preparing to leave, Liz handed Flanagan a note on a piece of writing paper. She had inscribed it with a quill in advance, just in case she met someone interesting. She liked being prepared when she was man hunting.

"Here's our address in Columbia. I would really like it if you would call on me some time in the near future!"

Philip Flanagan wasted no time in making his first visit to woo Liz. She had him at "Hello." He even put off doing some important tasks to have time for his frequent journeys.

On every trip, Philip would visit in their home and take Liz on slow surrey rides about town. At times he would drive to the little park at Duck River for a box lunch.

He never seemed extremely liberal with gifts or money. But he always showed genuine feeling for her and at times would bring her fresh-cut flowers.

*Well, he's just a frugal man,* she reasoned.

Liz especially enjoyed the night drives, after dinner that summer, when the temperatures were pleasant and the setting sun hung lazily over the verdant hilltops to the west. Often he would bring his surrey to a halt and draw her lovingly to his bosom—especially when no one else was near. He hungered for more, but was cautious not to seem too lustful.

The months flew by that summer. On Saturday night, August 27th, after he had gracefully asked for her hand, Philip felt her heart throbbing against his chest as he kissed her. He could never have realized that it was the anticipation of getting into his money box which excited her the most.

Polly planned a fairly fine wedding, not like a first one, for her daughter, but nice enough and it was held at the little rural Miller's Baptist Church, where she and Adam were both members, on 3 October 1831.

Liz immediately moved into Philip Flanagan's white weather-boarded house beside the carriage factory in Huntsville. She had always wanted a white picket fence since she had left home as a toddler. They had one in Maryland, and she vaguely remembered bumping into it and skinning her knee. Not a great thing to lodge in a memory bank, but it was what made her pay attention to it later.

Liz took Joshua and Sadie with her into her new life, and it pleased Philip a lot that she did so, since the good smithy could look after his equines and those of his friends. Liz thought it a bit strange, however, that he had no slaves of his own.

Things seemed to be going smoothly enough, but she noticed right away that Philip acted awfully secretive about his business and finances.

*I have to know exactly what I'm going to get out of this risky venture*, Liz thought.

So one day in early December she slyly watched out of the corner of her eye as he hid the key for the middle drawer in his roll top desk where she had seen him place his financial ledger.

That day, while Philip was at work in his factory, Elizabeth checked out the desk drawer. Lo and behold, she discovered that her new hubby was very severely indebted and the hole that he was digging for himself was getting deeper by the day!

*No money, no man!* she said to herself. This was not her first rodeo!

Mysteriously, Philip was soon stricken by what his doctor called "a strange illness."

He must appear to have a slow death, since they had only been married for such a short while. But she was learning the fine art of disappearing husbandry, and had discovered the advantage of tiny bits of hemlock.

For the next 90 days he consulted his physician 45 times; that is to say, every other day.

On 14 March 1832 Liz found her poor Phillip dead in his bed. His "grieving widow" had him laid to rest on his land near his factory. It was of course, a Liz only graveside affair.

She had the following inscription carved on his stone: "He was the sincear Friend, the agreeable companion, affectionate husband, the honest man."

Unfortunately, the engraver had not only misspelled 'sincere,' but had also spelled his name incorrectly on the stone marker. Liz made no effort to have it changed, though. What was the difference? He was dead anyway. Dead men don't talk, or care what is on their stones.

His children, however, were furious and later had his remains removed to Maple Hill Cemetery in Huntsville, a proper site where distinguished men were buried.

Elizabeth had no choice but to return to Columbia. Her sympathetic parents once again graciously opened their home to her.

She must now find a surefire way to climb the ladder to greater riches. This was downright disgusting!

Luckily for her, it wasn't long until she met the rich and powerful Alexander Jeffries. He was merely in the wrong place at the right time, visiting his son in Columbia and checking on his property there.

# Chapter Twenty-three

## Fall 1832: Columbia, Tennessee

**"T**ell me about yourself, young lady!" Alexander said to Elizabeth, as his eyes lit on her creamy cleavage. She dearly loved fine clothes and had dressed very seductively to meet him that day.

After learning about Jeffries from Ed, who had conducted business deals with him at the bank where he was now working, Liz had attended a social function at which the wealthy cotton planter was also certain to be present.

Liz knew that Jeffries was 60 years of age, and she, only 38, but what are a few years when a wagon load of money is involved?

"Well, where do I start, Alex," she said in a sensual tone. "My papa is quite the military hero! Not only did he serve with distinction by heading up a band of young boys in the War for Independence, but also commanded a large battalion of men under General Jackson in the War of 1812 and the Creek Indian War."

"Remarkable, Elizabeth! What a heritage! Were you born around these parts?" Southern gentleman that he was, Jeffries didn't bother to mention his own distinguished record of service to the country.

"No, sir. I was born up in Maryland, right next to the Atlantic Ocean. We came south when I was just a child, though. My mama gave me a good education. I've never had to do without anything and I have always gotten pretty much what I wanted."

Alex raised his bushy brows, his thin mouth curling to one side. Stroking his coarse mustache gently, he managed to muster an amused look. "I can just imagine!" he laughed.

They talked on awhile about the natural beauty of the Maury County area and what foods they each enjoyed most. They were pleased to find that a lot of their favorite dishes were the same.

Alex pulled a long Cuban cigar out of his inside jacket pocket, bit off the end and lit it.

"What was that?"

"You mean what did I use to light my cigar with?" Alex grinned.

"Yes! I've never seen such a thing in all my born days!"

Alex grinned bigger.

"It's called a friction light. It ignites with white prosperous. It was invented by a pharmacist over in England. This type is called a 'Lucifer.'"

"You mean like the devil?"

"Somebody's been in church!"

Liz's eyes opened wide.

"Uh, yes, my first husband was a preacher. I'm very familiar with Lucifer!"

*I just bet you are!* were the words which formed in Alex's mind.

"A friend of mine from London brought these strikes over. They'll be a big thing here in the states before you can say Jack Robinson! My friend is going to make sure that they are!"

"I would certainly think they will!"

"Now let's change the subject! I don't want to talk about smokes and lights.

"I'd very much like to get to know you, young lady," he said, taking a long puff on his cigar, "but I think you need to be aware of the fact that I have been married and my wife passed away a while back."

Jeffries' first wife, Frances, had died on 16 September 1825, at the age of 52. She had been buried on their plantation there at Hazel Green—the start of a family cemetery. The two had benefited from a joyful marriage and had given birth to three healthy children who were now grown and managing his other properties. Since he had been a widower for several years now, he was lonely and had a genuine desire to move on with his life.

"Well, sir, it's the same for me. I guess we have a great deal in common," Liz answered. "My last husband once owned a small plantation which he had sold before I met him to start a carriage factory, but we weren't married very long when he passed away and it was willed to his family."

"Well, my lady, I own a *large* plantation in Madison County, Alabama and a great deal more land here in Tennessee and down in Mississippi as well! I would love to have the honor of taking you out to dinner tonight at The Downtown Café where all the mule breeders go to dine. My son is one of them! It is getting to be quite a large industry here in Columbia."

"I have not the slightest interest in mules, kind sir," Liz smiled demurely, "but I would truly love to have dinner with you this evening!"

"Well, I thought you might also be interested in hearing that James K. Polk has been known to eat there quite a few times, as well. He's a Congressman up in Washington, you know!"

Liz was very familiar with Polk. She had always made it her business to know who was who in society.

*Now this is the stuff the good life is made of!*

Liz moved away a little and her mouth widened. Her smile was one that would have melted any man's heart.

"Then it's a date! Pick me up at six and don't be late!" she exclaimed, giving him her address and flipping her silky hair to one side.

That night when Jeffries' shiny surrey pulled up at the Dale home, Liz was staring excitedly out the window. She didn't want to seem too anxious, so she waited until he banged the large brass knocker on their front door.

Her mystical smile warmly welcomed him.

"Won't you come in, Alex?" she said sensuously.

"No thanks, my lady! We need to get going! Time's a wastin'!"

Liz grinned widely, told her mother 'so long' and bounded out to his fashionable waiting surrey.

It turned out that Polk was on a sabbatical from Washington and he and his wife were at the café that very evening. Quickly spotting him, Alex grasped Liz's dainty hand and strolled boldly over to the Congressman's table.

"Congressman Polk, I hope you remember me. Alexander Jeffries? I helped you in your campaign for Congress. I was in Columbia at the time, if you recall."

Polk looked at Alex for only a few seconds and his lips began to curl.

"Oh yes, of course I remember you! How have you been getting on, my good man?"

"Just spiffy, your honor! I just wanted to introduce you to my date, the lovely widow Flanagan!"

Polk's hand went out for Liz's, gently pulling the back of it to his puckered lips.

Liz grinned like the Cheshire cat.

"So pleased to meet you, my lady! Would you both like to join Sarah and me for dinner?"

Before the enchanted Liz had the slightest chance to open her mouth, Jeffries spoke his piece.

"Well, thank you so much, sir, but this is our first date, and we would like to have this time just for ourselves, if you know what I mean."

Polk bowed his stately head slightly to hide his awkward grin.

"I certainly do, my friend. Y'all have a great time, now, you hear?"

Liz had been captivated with Polk from the very moment she laid eyes on him.

After dinner, Alex took Liz for a lengthy ride around town while they got to know one another more intimately. When they arrived back at the Dale home it was growing quite late. A screech owl hooted and flew out of the large oak at the side of the house.

Removing his black top hat, Alex pulled her close for a long, passionate kiss. He was sure that he saw fireworks exploding around them. Liz was just as certain that she could see shiny coins of gold and silver twirling about her dreamy cranium.

That night was the beginning of their storybook courtship. But Liz would always draw back when Alex got too close to trying to make love to her. He wasn't like Flanagan. She wanted to dig her claws in deep before she gave him her body. She needed to make sure that he knew she was playing for keeps.

Had Alexander had any inkling of the manner in which her former husbands had died, he may have been more cautious. But when it came to Elizabeth, there was just something strangely bewitching about her that was a powerful magnet to men of all ages.

# Chapter Twenty-four

## Spring 1833: Columbia, Tennessee

"**Y**ou say this fellow, Jeffries, has a plantation down in Hazel Green, Alabama?" Adam asked, holding his clean-shaven chin in his left hand.

"Yes indeedie!" Liz said proudly, raring back her auburn head. "He's quite well-to-do!"

"That I don't doubt! I have something else I need to talk to this man about, though! The next time he comes to court you I want to meet him. Let me know ahead of time and I'll make sure I'm home!"

"Well, I can tell you right now, Papa, he's coming this Friday evening!"

"Just make sure he stays here for dinner. Have Sadie fix him something special. That way I can get to know him."

"I will, Papa, I will!"

But the ladies of the house decided not to use Sadie for cooking this special dinner. Polly and

Liz, themselves, prepared a scrumptious meal of rainbow trout, turnip greens, mashed potatoes, white beans, coleslaw, onions and cornbread, and sliced some vine-ripened tomatoes to set it off. Pecan pie was baked for dessert.

"My, my! You have outdone yourselves, ladies! You made this all by yourselves, did you?" Alex exclaimed as he was ushered to the table by a smiling Sadie.

Polly tried not to act overly proud and just pushed a light simper across her charming face.

"Just the two of us," Liz said, not giving "a tinker's dam" how it sounded, as were her words at times like this.

There was a lot of idle chatter at the dinner table that night. Adam was greatly impressed with Liz's latest beau, even though he was nearer his own age than hers. He could hardly wait until they had finished eating and had retired to the parlor to have his discussion. But wait he did.

"Alex, ole boy," he began, "I understand that you have a plantation down in Hazel Green, just over the Alabama line, am I correct?"

"That you are, sir! It's quite a nice place. Come down see me soon! I understand that you fought in the Creek Indian War. You must have been down my way at that time, at least."

Alex had opened the door, now he was going to waltz right in.

"Yep! That's the very reason I brought it up! Do you have any idea who named your quaint little town?"

"I've always heard that it was President Jackson, but that was a little before my time there, so I couldn't swear to anything."

"Right you are, Alex! Now let me tell you exactly how that happened. Back then he was our General, of course. The General, I still call him that, was marching all of his troops from Fayetteville down into Alabama to fight the Indians in the fall of '13. It was before we went to Dadesville where the Battle of Horseshoe Bend was fought. I was commanding 100 of those troops. We had been marching non-stop that day and a lot of my older men were just plain tuckered out. When we got into your area I asked the General if I could stop there for the night to give my men a much-needed rest. He didn't act at first like he was paying much attention to me.

"There were a lot of Hazel bushes along the road and they were the brightest shade of green I believe I ever saw.

"The General just looked me straight in the eye and said, 'I think this place ought to be called Hazel Green, don't you, Captain Dale?'

"Now you know if you ever met the General that you didn't argue with him.

"'That sounds like a jam up idea to me, sir!' I said.

"That's when I knew he had heard my request. He gave me permission to stay the night there, so I found a peaceful spot and me and my men encamped beside a big spring just to the south, close to Meridianville. He took the rest of the troops on down to Huntsville before they made camp.

"The next morning I shared what Jackson had said to me with the locals who had stopped by to bid us Godspeed. They must have told everybody they knew! I reckon it stuck!"

Alex listened very carefully to his every word, occasionally nodding.

"That's a mighty interesting story there, Adam. One which I shall never forget! They were already calling it Hazel Green when I bought my land and moved there in 1818. They made it official in '21, if I recall correctly.

Alex was definitely hooked. Liz was about to reel in her first really big fish!

# Chapter Twenty-five

## November 1833: Columbia, Tennessee

**W**ednesday 6 November 1833 was a date that Alex Jeffries had been hankering for for over a year! In fact, he'd been marking off each day on his lithograph wall calendar with an X.

He arrived at the First Methodist Church of Columbia almost an hour early.

Elizabeth scurried around like a squirrel scavenging for nuts to store for winter, trying to make sure that she could be at the church on time. This wasn't like just going to church on Sunday morning! Adam wasn't helping any by his constant prodding, either. Polly had made her a lovely white gingham wedding gown almost as pretty as the form it adorned.

Liz's sister, Sophie, who had married Robert Turner before leaving Liberty, had agreed to be her Matron of Honor, and her daughter, Mahala and Ed's daughters Anne and young Mary served as her bridesmaids.

That glorious day, he and Elizabeth were married in a sweeping ceremony with all the gallantry of aristocracy.

Ed's wife, Frances, had insisted on helping plan this wedding, especially since she was familiar with the church and was a good friend of the pastor and his family. Alex had wanted to share the expense, but Adam had been adamant about paying for everything!

Alex stood beside the minister, as still as a marble statue, in a stunning black tuxedo with a lacy white shirt and black string bow tie. The entire entourage was dressed to the nines.

The large edifice was packed with friends and relatives on both sides. There were even a few in attendance from Liberty whom Adam and Polly had invited. The massive pipe organ began to play Canon in D, as requested by Alex, and Adam began marching stoically up the aisle holding his magnificent daughter by the hand. All eyes were fixed upon them.

"We are gathered here today in the sight of God and this company to unite this man and this woman in the holy state of matrimony..."

Alex looked over at Liz as if he could eat her up.

"Marriage is not by any to be entered into unadvisedly or lightly; but reverently, discreetly, advisedly, soberly, and in the fear of God. Marriages are made in heaven and consummated on earth."

Liz held her comments but wished for an end to this boring ceremony. Heaven, huh? She knew she had to say 'I do,' to get what she wanted, but the words of the preacher made her cringe.

Finally, the service came to a conclusion. No one objected, and the two were legally wed.

And of course, Elizabeth retained Joshua and Sadie.

Alex was overly thrilled to have his own black-smith now, and soon had a well-equipped shop set up for Joshua adjoining the fancy stables a ways to the rear of the house at the edge of the pasture. There were already some basic smithing tools there in a barn that had been used by a hired hand for emergencies. He had never been able to use them properly and Alex had sent him packing after he had injured one of his horses.

They spent their two-week honeymoon in Alex's cozy two-story log cabin on the back of the

Indian mound—others were forbidden to enter except for the servants who prepared their meals and cleaned the house. Sally, Alex's beautiful head cook, showed Liz's Sadie the ropes and the two of them did the lion's share of the housework, with some aid from a sixty-two-year-old male named Jacob.

Alexander was in hog heaven and Elizabeth was laughing up her puffy sleeve. But she knew that she had to keep him happy and prosperous long enough to inherit the property at Hazel Green. No more Flanagan shenanigans!

Each day she would make herself rise early, have Sally prepare their breakfast and treat her husband with the utmost respect; lots of candy kisses and sufficient love making at night to keep him under her spell. She made it all so believable!

After about four months of marriage, she awoke him one cool March morning with a warm, fervent kiss.

"You must be kind to me, Darling. I have every reason to believe that we will soon be welcoming a dear little one into our home!"

"Oh, my love! That's wonderful news! I pray that you are right about that!"

Liz could feel the genuine anticipation in Alex's coarse masculine voice.

# 1834

Alex had whistled each morning as he went about his work. He was a changed man. He was kind to the slaves and treated Liz like an angel.

Surely enough, in less than a year after they were married, Liz began her labor and asked Alex to go after the only midwife in their tiny town, a plump thirty-plus-year-old, widowed nurse named Barbara Hazel.

She didn't have to ask twice! Within three hours after the midwife arrived, a tiny red-faced son, William Alexander Jeffries was born, kicking and screaming.

Of course the house must be enlarged. Or maybe a new one should be built? Yes! She decided right then and there; that is definitely what she would have!

# *Chapter Twenty-six*

## 1835: Columbia, Tennessee

"**H**ello, I'm Nathan Vaught. Your brother has told me an awfully lot about you." The smartly dressed Vaught took off his shiny black top hat and bowed courteously.

Sarah Dale smiled, though ever so slightly. Like her feisty older sister, she was very fair to look upon, but at 33 years of age she had never been married. She was appalled at the way Liz had treated her husbands and as a result, was shy around all men.

"Your brother told me that he would introduce us but...oh, there he is now!"

Sarah had visited the First Methodist Church today at the request of Ed. She might have known that he had an ulterior motive!

"Is this your doings, Ed? Really?"

Ed looked at her with an awkward smirk.

"You'll like Nate, Sarah, dear. Just give him a chance. He's the most gracious man I have ever known, next to Papa."

Vaught gazed at Liz sympathetically.

"I thought you were aware that Ed had spoken to me about you; my sincere apologies, milady."

Nathan nodded and was about to walk away when a young lassie toddled up looking like the child of royalty.

"Hello, madam, how are you today? You are very pretty!" Then she curtsied.

Sarah peered down and her heart dissolved. The little one had the face of an angel and was dressed like she had just wandered out of a fashion shop. Kneeling at the girl's side she addressed her softly:

"Well, hello, young princess! What's your name?"

"Mary Jane, what's yours?"

"Sarah! Is this gentleman your papa?"

"Uh-huh. My mommy's gone to heaven. But Papa is a wonderful man. I love him so much!" Her head was wagging and her eyes held deep earnestness.

Sarah stood and looked for the first time directly into the face of Nathan Vaught. She saw the same innocence and honesty that she was seeing in the child.

"Perhaps we should start over," she said, reaching out to shake Vaught's hand.

"May I buy you some lunch?" Nate said tenderly.

"But of course."

As they ate that day, Nathan asked Sarah to tell him about herself. She, being shy and unpretentious, just told him the basics of where she was from and how she ended up in Columbia because of Ed. Afterward, he related his own fascinating life story to her.

"I was born 12 August 1799 in the Shenandoah Valley of Virginia. I had one brother, Joseph.

"While I was but a small child, my parents moved to Rutherford County, in the very center of the state of Tennessee. My dear mother died only two years after the move; then my father departed this life two years later.

"My brother and I were placed in foster care with a couple named Radford who soon moved us to Columbia. When Mrs. Radford also passed away, at my age 11, my brother and I were split up. I was bound out to a cabinetmaker named James Purcell to learn the trade. In 1811, Purcell began building houses. Ten years later, he died and I took over the business. People liked my work because I tried so hard to please them. I wanted desperately to be the best in the business. Soon I was able to start attracting wealthy clients. I owe my gift to the Almighty."

Sarah was intent and taken aback.

"I've been blessed to be able to build some of the finest homes and businesses here in Maury County. In fact, I supervised the construction of our church building."

"Oh, my! I had no idea!"

"My team, under my supervision, has recently started work on a structure now being called 'The Athenaeum' downtown. It was originally meant to be the home of Samuel Polk Walker, the nephew of James K. Polk, but he got married and moved out of state. It has now been selected to serve as the Rectory for the Columbia Female Institute, a Christian school."

Sarah sighed. She was almost speechless. When she collected her thoughts she asked: "And what happened to the mother of your little princess."

"It's still just so hard for me to talk about, Sarah. I married a wonderful lady. Her name was Lucretia. I thought she would be with me the rest of my life. In '34 she came down with cholera. She had just given birth to our second daughter, Virginia. Lucretia passed away in my arms. The baby died the very next day."

Tears welled up in Nathan's eyes, though he tried so hard to hold them back.

"I am so sorry, Nate! I can't even imagine how you must have felt. I have lost some close family members, but a spouse and a child…at the same time?" Sarah reached for his hands and choked back her own emotions.

Sarah agreed that day to begin seeing Nathan on a regular basis. She could feel his pain and his deep, genuine love. But it was young Mary Jane who truly sealed the deal between them. Someone who could have brought this child into the world and gained her love and respect in such a genuine way had to be a very special man.

They had met in early March. The couple was married in May that year in the First Methodist Church and Sarah also became a member there.

Nathan had become known as the "Master Builder of Columbia" and supervised the erection of the most prestigious homes in the area including Rattle and Snap, Clifton Place, Elm Springs, Hamilton Place, Fairmont and many more.

He also was in charge of construction of The State Bank in Columbia, where Ed was now employed.

# 1836

The couple's first child was born about ten months later, on 4 March 1836. In honor of her father, Sarah christened him, Adam Dale Vaught. Adam was fit to be tied, he was so proud!

That year Nathan oversaw the building of the new First Methodist Church building on West 7th Street.

# 1837

The fabulous Athenaeum was completed in 1837 and featured both Gothic and Moorish architectural elements. Nathan felt that this unique splendid structure was a monument to his new-found happiness. Especially given the use it would have.

It was that year when Nathan built the Elms Spring Mansion, another Greek revival home near Columbia on the stage road leading from Pulaski to Franklin.

Sarah had truly found her place in the world. She certainly realized that the family's move to Columbia had been most providential in her life.

But down the road in Hazel Green, Alabama, a separate string of events was in progress.

The cotton plantation was doing exceptionally well. The 1837 bumper crop was harvested by the slaves in September for another season.

Then in November 1837, a daughter was also added to the Jeffries family. Liz named her Mary Elizabeth after herself and her mother, Mary "Polly" Dale. She must stay in control of the estate and preserve it for her own children.

But the wheels inside Elizabeth's pretty head were shrewdly turning. She had now convinced Alexander to will the Hazel Green plantation and the land in Mississippi to her and their children. There was plenty of property in Tennessee for his older children.

# *Chapter Twenty-seven*
## 1838: Hazel Green, Alabama

"**I** went to visit with my sister last week who lives just a few miles south of here near the Flint River. As I got close to her house I could see an army captain who was driving a great big bunch of Indians who were in wretched condition. When I got inside her house, my sister told me that they'd been camped there for the last two nights. She said that they had been marched there to the river from Chattanooga and that they were Cherokees. They were all filthy dirty and some of 'em had their clothes torn half off! Shoot, several of 'em were bleeding pretty bad! Those poor Indians had been beaten so much and were so bony thin that I bet some of 'em died right there in that camp!"

It was Sunday, July 1st, 1838 and a lady named Carol was talking to Liz after church while several other women stood around with their mouths open.

You know, to Elizabeth, church services were merely a societal function. She had found that several of her neighbors were attending the Meridianville Cumberland Presbyterian Church in Hazel Green which had been formed there in 1807 before it had become a separate town. It was one of the earliest organized congregations in the new breakaway denomination which had been structured in Tennessee. She couldn't dare take a chance on missing out on getting to know the well-healed ladies of Hazel Green, so she made it a point to be there with bells on every Sunday morning.

Carol's eyes danced like skilled ballerinas as she flung her hands rapidly about while she was relating her heartrending story.

"I heard that they're all being taken out to Oklahoma Territory to a permanent homeland," one woman said who was also standing by with her ears pealed.

"Oh, yes! My sister told me that. But they had to give up their ancestral lands! What I saw there was downright awful!" Carol said, grimacing. "They were being forced to get onto a big boat before I left! I just can't believe that our own government could be so cruel."

"Good riddance of bad redskins!" Liz mumbled as she walked slowly away.

Liz thought no more about the incident, except for recalling what her father had said about the Indian Removal Act a few years earlier.

That summer was a very lovely one, indeed, in picturesque North Alabama. Not too much rain, and temperatures were most often in the eighties Fahrenheit for highs.

Elizabeth took almost as much pleasure in horseback riding as she did in hosting festive parties. She had selected a sleek, chestnut-colored Tennessee Walker mare, with a white flame-like mark on her forehead, as her own, and had named her Blaze. Naturally, she had received no flack at all from her dear Alex, who always tried his dead level best to please her, unless the request was too far-fetched.

One day in mid-August she had Joshua tack Blaze up and fairly flew through the grassy pasture behind the stables adjoining the cotton fields. Then she opened the big rail gate and rode like the wind on across the lovely green meadow with the summer breeze whipping on her face and blowing back her hair. How marvelously free she felt!

Passing by a placid pond, she cautiously ventured on into the wooded area on the south end of the plantation. A rustling in the low brush brought out a startled doe and two young spotted fawns which had obviously been born that spring.

*What gorgeous beauties!* she thought. Then suddenly, from behind a copse of trees, a large timber rattler emerged, tail aloft and shaking; in striking position!

Liz softly clicked her tongue and slowly backed Blaze away, turning the reins to go back toward home. Her heart was pounding like a bongo.

*Why didn't I bring a shotgun?* she wondered.

She realized immediately that she must be careful! Her dreams were too close to fruition. But Alex loved his old log cabin and had made it clear to her that he wasn't of a mind to have a bigger house built. Here is where he drew the line! Well, she knew how to draw too.

That evening Liz told Alex of her daunting escapade in heightened tones.

"You'll have to be more cautious, my dear! You shouldn't wander into those woods! There are a lot of bad critters out there, not just snakes! Things like wolves, for instance!"

"You're right, you know. I'll stay away from those woods on my future outings. But you know how much I love being out riding in this divine weather!"

Alex nodded and smiled, pulling her in for a suggestive kiss.

"Speaking of bad critters," Elizabeth said, pushing back, her pleasant expression quickly changing to a frown, "of late I've noticed a big rat running across the kitchen floor!"

"Perhaps we should bring one of the barn cats inside."

"I can't tolerate cats in the house, I am allergic to them. I can pick up some rat poison when I go to the store."

And the next day, she did just that. The "rat" was never brought up again.

On 14 September, one of the young male slaves who had been working harvesting cotton came dashing into the house. His tone was frantic, his voice shaking, his eyes wide and wild.

"It's Massa! Ma'am! It's Massa! He's a-layin' dead out by da big barn! When I seed him it scared the bigjesus out of me, ma'am! What should I do?"

"Have Jacob help you, Toby. Bring Mr. Jeffries in the house."

When Alexander was laid out on his bed, his body was swollen all over; his fingernails and toenails appeared yellow. His tongue had turned thick and black.

Liz calmly told Sadie to clean him up and change his underwear and trousers.

The very thought of having to do such a thing made Sadie feel like throwing up, but she knew better than to refuse any of Liz's requests. She knew they weren't really requests, but demands.

That night Elizabeth went to their cabins, woke up a few slaves and ordered them to bury Alex immediately in the cemetery near the back of the house.

"It will keep the disease from spreading," she told them glumly.

Jacob, Toby and Joshua dug a four-foot-deep hole, as quickly as possible, next to his first wife's gravestone, wrapped their master's stiffening body in a heavy bed sheet and laid him to rest as the household servants, Sally and Sadie, stood by Elizabeth, looking on with straight faces. The only tears were those of the frightened slaves.

The Jeffries' servants spread the word of what had happened to those of their neighbors, who informed their own masters and the condition of his unsightly body was reported in the *Huntsville Advocate*.

At church, hushed murmurs were swiftly spreading around. A doctor in Huntsville had stated that these were signs of arsenic poisoning. The corpse had already been laid to rest and no one had an ounce of proof.

What could anyone do?

The children cried and cried, until they seemed to have no more tears left in them.

Liz visited the bank the next day and learned that Alex and his son in Tennessee were the only authorized signers on the plantation accounts. With angry words spewed at the bank manager, she immediately opened a new account in her own name, but knew that she was starting over.

Life would go on on the Jeffries plantation at
Hazel Green. But for the slaves, it would be more
brutal than ever.

# Chapter Twenty-eight

## November 1, 1838: Hazel Green, Alabama

**O**ut behind the smokehouse the once lovely and graceful cook, Sally, was facing against the dull grayness of the weathered building; her arms extended upward, her dress ripped off and her tender breasts bare upon the rough boards.

Her shrill screams could have been heard far into the stubble fields left from the harvest of the cotton as the cold leather tips ripped deep into the tender flesh of her back. Blood was flowing down Sally's torso and legs onto the ground. Elizabeth, herself, wielded the riding crop which was meant to only crack in the air to spur the horses onward when need be.

Sally had overslept after serving at a Halloween ball late the night before at which Elizabeth's friends had been guests. Though the expression was not used in that day, the principle certainly was. Liz had what we know as a "zero tolerance" policy for servants not being on time for needed chores or to prepare meals, as the case had been this morning.

*These niggers have to learn who's boss around here!* she thought. *Sally will be an example to any of the others who have any doubts about my supreme authority!*

She jerked the cruel whip backward for the tenth time and let it rip again.

As if she hadn't made her sovereign rule painfully clear. Her commands had always been fierce and terrorizing.

Sally wondered if Liz resented her more because she was so beautiful or because Alex had shown her preference. Perhaps it was both.

Liz had invited ladies from as far away as Columbia to attend her costume party. And of course, the husbands of the married ones. Two of them had spent the night in the log home. But there just wasn't enough room for everyone. A new roomy and luxurious mansion was what she needed. She would certainly have to do something about that. She would find herself a new rich husband!

Before long little William would need to be schooled, so she began inquiring about men with connections to education in the state of Alabama. Specifically eligible ones with money.

"There's a dashing gentleman in Limestone County," her best friend Anna told her while having coffee that afternoon, "who has served in the State Legislature for the past two years. He's a great advocate of common schools."

She had found that she and Anna had a lot in common; both were devious and greedy. And she knew that she could count on Anna's confidentiality.

"Hmmm! It that so? Are you certain that he isn't married?"

"He definitely is not. As a matter of fact, he's seeking his fourth wife now!"

A broad grin came over Elizabeth's cunning, meditative face.

"I hope you won't mind that he's a bit bald. He makes a lot of effort to hide it, though, with his side hair and his stylish hat!"

"What difference does that make? I've heard that bald men are actually more virile!"

Both women broke out in hilarious laughter, continuing to sip their hot java.

"I have a good friend in Athens who knows him personally that I can contact to introduce you, if you wish," Anna said. "The gentleman's name is Robert High."

"Indeed? Please do so, and with the utmost haste! He wants a wife, does he? Let's not keep him waiting!"

# *Chapter Twenty-nine*

## December 1838: Hazel Green, Alabama

**W**ithin a fortnight a telegram had arrived at the Jeffries' house. Liz was ecstatic. A meeting had been arranged in Huntsville after the holidays with the Honorable Congressman High.

Meanwhile, Christmas was quickly approaching and Liz had heard her friends at church talking about the fabulous new children's poem, *A Visit with St. Nicholas,* written by Clemet Moore. It was now available as a picture book from New York, they said, so she had ordered a copy for William and Mary Beth, as she called her lovely little girl.

*This will be their Christmas gift; they'll both feel great about me!* she reasoned.

The week before Christmas she picked up the book at the post office and she read it to them that night at bedtime.

"'Twas the night before Christmas, when all through the house

"Not a creature was stirring, not even a mouse;

"The stockings were hung by the chimney with care,
In hopes that St. Nicholas soon would be there;

"The children were nestled all snug in their beds,
While visions of sugar-plums danced in their heads;

"And mamma in her 'kerchief, and I in my cap,
Had just settled our brains for a long winter's nap,

"When out on the lawn there arose such a clatter,
I sprang from the bed to see what was the matter.

"Away to the window I flew like a flash,
Tore open the shutters and threw up the sash…"

"Who is Saint Nick-lus, Mommy?" Mary Beth interrupted.

Liz stumbled with her reply. She sensed trouble.

"W-well, he's a jolly old elf who brings toys to children at Christmas."

"Then how come we don't get anything from him at Christmas, Mama?" William asked quizzically.

"You will this year, little one," she nodded reluctantly. "He has just found out where you live. You see, he lives up at the North Pole and he has to fly all over the world in his sleigh. There are lots and lots of boys and girls and he has to learn where they all live!"

"Oh goodie, Mommy!" Mary Beth said excitedly!

"Well, he only brings gifts to good little boys and girls. So you both have to be really good!"

Liz finished reading the poem, laid the book down on the table and changed the subject.

*I would be flat out of luck if I were a child and there really was a Santa Claus,* she thought. *Why did I have to order that damned book?*

But the next week she forced herself to get out and buy small toys for the children. A little horn and blocks for William and a dolly and clothes for Mary Beth.

Little Mary Elizabeth had visions of sugar-plums dancing in her head while Mama Elizabeth had visions of silver coins being spent for nonsense that could have been used for her own benefit.

# Chapter Thirty

## 1839: Hazel Green, Alabama

As Liz's sleek *Flanagan Surrey* rolled into Huntsville at 11:00 o'clock that cool January morning, pulled by her exquisite Blaze, she began to hear the clinking of other horses' hooves against the hardened streets. She was soon passing more and more warmly-wrapped people going about their business in the small, fashionable city.

The beautiful courthouse, where the meeting was scheduled to occur, had just been built less than three years earlier. It had replaced the one built in 1818 and was the first Greek revival style building in Huntsville. Liz thought it was striking in appearance. But it reminded her too much of Nathan Vaught and as she looked at it, she was more determined than ever to have a house at least on the level of her sister's.

As she reined her beautiful Blaze in toward the courthouse hitching rail, she heard a man's high-pitched voice calling out her name.

"Yoo-hoo! Mrs. Jeffries!" The average height, handsome, balding man was rushing toward her from across the busy street.

"That must mean that you are the Honorable Congressman High!"

"That I am; that I am!" came the warm reply, "but to you, fair lady, I am merely 'Robbie.' I'm so glad that I was informed of the appearance of the horse and surrey you'd be driving!"

Liz smiled.

"May I drive you to the livery?"

"Why, yes! Thank you, kind sir."

Liz slid over and handed Robbie the reigns.

"Can we get some lunch?" she asked sweetly.

"Why, certainly!"

As they lunched that day at a fancy café, Liz learned that High was from a family of the bourgeois, originally from North Carolina. This lawyer-politician was just who she had been looking for!

Liz rambled on and on, expounding to him about her own exciting adventuresome past and noble ancestry. She was a descendant of Cecil Calvert, Lord Baltimore, she told him.

High was much less braggadocios, but there were some interesting factors about his past that she would simply have to wait awhile to discover.

Twice every month, on Saturday, they met in Huntsville and had dinner at the town's finest establishments. What a sharp contrast between him and Flanagan! He was much more like Alex!

Liz didn't have a magic wand, per se, but she undoubtedly had some highly unusual qualities. It didn't take long for the accomplished cowgirl to pull in the lonesome congressman with her charm rope.

It was a match made somewhere besides in heaven, but the couple was married at the church which High attended in Athens on 15 May 1839. It had been a short engagement and High had asked for a simple ceremony. Liz just wanted to get it over with, so she had heartily agreed.

And yes, High moved onto the plantation with her and assumed the role of master! But maybe she could now get her new home!

During that year's gubernatorial campaign, she was delighted to learn that her new husband was an actual personal friend of James K. Polk's. Polk was also from the same area of North Carolina as Robbie, Mecklenburg County, and their families had been in touch for a good many years.

That fall they journeyed up to Columbia to Polk's home to celebrate with him and his team when he was elected Governor of Tennessee.

"James, or should I call you 'Young Hickory' now?" Robbie smiled. Leaning over slightly, he lifted a sparkling glass of Champaign for a toast that had just been proposed by the incoming governor's campaign manager.

Polk returned his smile as he took a brief sip from his shiny crystal goblet.

"Huh! I think it's kind of cute that people refer to me by that moniker now! You know what a follower of Jackson I've always been. Actually, he was my mentor. But you should still call me James, like you always did!"

"Anyway, *James*," I believe you have already met my lovely wife, Elizabeth. She tells me that she was introduced to you at the Downtown Café some years back when she was with the late Alex Jeffries, God rest his soul."

Polk squinted, grunted; then his eyes widened.

"Oh, yes!" Polk chuckled. "Now I remember! I was home on a visit from Washington! My Land o' Goshen, Robbie, how time does fly! That has been several years, but it seems but yesterday! Your wife is she? Congratulations, old boy! You certainly lassoed a beautiful filly!"

Elizabeth grinned sheepishly.

*Who lassoed whom?* But she couldn't help but like the metaphor anyway!

"I have a lovely mare..." Liz interrupted, "a Tennessee Walker which my late husband, Alex, told me came from just down the road from here in Shelbyville. I call her Blaze! I truly love to ride! Perhaps you could find a little time to visit us some day. It would be my pleasure to go on a trot around our plantation with you! We have a lot of horses in our stables and a large pasture. I'd love to show it all to you!"

From her tone of voice Polk wondered exactly what she might include in "all." But he let it slide.

"Not sure about that, my lady!" Polk had a tiny frown developing on his brow. "Politics keeps me hopping. But it would be wonderful, no doubt! I'm afraid that being Governor of Tennessee is going to be a full-time job!"

Liz continued to beam. "Well, you know you are welcome anytime."

"Make sure you get enough Champagne," Polk continued, "or if you prefer, we have some Blanton's Kentucky Bourbon! It just came out this year, but I have a friend from Kentucky who brought me a quart of it just for this occasion. He's here somewhere," he said, looking around. "Prohibition started in Tennessee last year and you can't buy it in the stores."

"We'll just stick to the bubbly, James. Thanks so much, though. My heartiest congratulations on your amazing victory! You can go a long way in the political arena! You might even be President of these United States some day!"

Polk laughed.

"Don't count on it, but thanks a lot for your vote of confidence, anyway, my friend! That gives me something to mull over for the future, I guess."

"By the by," Liz said, "speaking of President Jackson, as you were a while ago, my papa commanded men under him in the last war! I never had the pleasure of meeting the man, but Papa always spoke very highly of him."

"I'm glad to hear it, Ms. Elizabeth! He is certainly a national treasure!"

Then she thought for a second and spoke again, just to make conversation. "But Papa didn't like the Indian Removal. What did you think about that?"

Polk also waited a moment to respond; then said, "You know I was in Congress at the time that bill came up, and that was one of the hardest decisions we ever had to make. I felt when we voted on it that it was the only thing we could do, but after I found out the way they were treated, I felt very badly about how it was carried out."

"Thank you for that," Robbie said. "I was against it from the very beginning; but, of course I had no say in the matter. I understand the position you were in, though."

Being Elizabeth's same age, Polk couldn't help being taken aback by her rare beauty and uncommon charm. But he knew a flirt when he saw one. And he wasn't the least interested in anyone but his wife.

Sarah Childress Polk was dashing about the parlor, mingling with the guests. From one of the most influential families in Tennessee, she had met her future husband at a very young age. They felt like they had known one another all of their lives. Their courtship had come much later.

Unfortunately, the couple had never been able to have children of their own and out of loneliness, she had fostered those of some of her relatives. Luckily, she had great hosting skills and had done a marvelous job with the present affair.

Elizabeth was enormously envious of Sarah Polk. Not only did she have the same given name as her high-browed sister; she had a sharp, handsome, powerful husband. One which was known far and wide and no doubt had a fabulous future.

Soon Robert's term in the State Legislature came to an end and his expensive reelection campaign failed. But he really didn't care at all. Actually he was somewhat relieved. He still had his law practice to keep him busy.

Elizabeth, however, continued to host a goodly number of communal events and was able to gain a few new socialite friends.

But the horror of what was soon to happen took her mind temporarily off of her jealousy and even her now more lack-luster social life.

# *Chapter Thirty-one*
## July 1840: Hazel Green, Alabama

On 8 July 1840, a youthful messenger came riding up to the mansion door. Elizabeth knew at once that something had gone horribly wrong.

"Telegram, ma'am," she heard the rider say most solemnly.

The tall, blond young man dismounted and stood as still as a soldier at attention, extending his left hand.

*Lefties are not a good sign either*, Liz thought.

She hurriedly grabbed the folded pale yellow paper; rapidly jerked it open and read its shocking message:

*Come home at once stop Edward has taken his own life stop Mother*

As callous as Liz was, large tears puffed up in her dark eyes and she reached out to grasp the delivery boy and pull him in for a desperately needed hug.

# Columbia, Tennessee

Upon arriving in Columbia, where Edward had been serving as a bank officer, justice of the peace and Trustee of the Methodist Church that Nathan had built, she was further astonished. Her dear, treasured brother had cut his own throat at the home of his close friend, John W. Fry. As an employee of The State Bank he had reportedly made a number of loans which had not been repaid as agreed. At any rate, it had been discovered that a great deal of money was missing that should have been in the bank.

Her mother was shaking like a leaf as she handed Liz the despondent suicide note that Edward had left proclaiming his innocence in the bank matter.

*I have nothing left to live for; I cannot be of any service to my family. It pains me to leave them in penury; it is also exceedingly painful to me to leave my friends involved to such an extent on my account—these things have been brought about by a combination of circumstances over which I had only partial control.*

Another bank officer wrote a statement for the permanent record which read:

*Edward W. Dale, being alone, did wickedly, unlawfully, and voluntarily kill himself by cutting his own throat.*

Then he callously placed the note in a box of inquests which was stored in the basement of the Maury County Court House.

Ed's children were bawling so hard at his funeral that they were hopelessly inconsolable. This seemed to Liz like the worst kind of déjà vu.

His older children insisted that Ed be buried next to their mother in Greenwood Cemetery. The grief-stricken Frances immediately agreed without thinking of objecting. She certainly didn't want to make enemies of Ed's children.

After the gloomy funeral, Elizabeth moped around for several days. It was the hardest thing she had ever been through. Though she would be heartbroken, she wasn't one to pout for the long haul. She had other matters to attend to.

# *Chapter Thirty-two*

## 1842: Hazel Green, Alabama

**"W**hy do you keep harassing me about building another house, Liz? The one we have now is plenty good enough! I didn't win in the last election and I don't care about all this highfalutin stuff anymore!" Robbie was obviously infuriated.

"Do you think I married you to stagnate in this boxy old cabin? Surely not! I need a suitable home! I love having parties and socializing! That's my life! You ought to know that by now!"

"Well, unless you have some other way of getting the money, you can just flat out forget it! I am the master of this plantation!"

Liz stormed out of the room and rushed to the stable for a much-needed ride on Blaze. She had to clear her angry head. Joshua was busy currying another horse, but he always stopped and did her bidding.

*The only decent thing that Robbie ever did was to get a school started in Meridianville and get William enrolled! But he doesn't know who he's fooling with. He wouldn't have this place if it weren't for me! It's really mine!*

Robert leaned back his bald head on his favorite arm chair and took a long draw off his pipe. He had grown dreadfully wary of Elizabeth's bombastic, power-hungry ways. Their initial spark, if they ever really had one, had dwindled to a dead ember.

Now it seemed that she was always out riding Blaze or gallivanting about the county in the surrey, meeting with her well-bred friends, while he was left alone at the plantation to prepare for his legal cases and see after the slaves. Though the servants were greatly relieved in her absence that just wasn't his cup of tea—or even coffee!

Two years had passed since Edward's death. Liz had to get her mind permanently off of what had nearly been the death of her.

Things just weren't moving quickly enough for the queen of the hill, though. She was able to redecorate the cabin for her entertaining, but what society lady wants to live in an outmoded log cabin? Since Robert obviously had no interest in building a fancy mansion any more than Alex had—or expanding his own social life—she would have to resort to plan B.

One sunny April morning, Robert began feeling strange and called for Liz, but she was nowhere to be found. She hadn't even told him that she was leaving. Sally was outside, talking with Jacob, so his cries were only heard by Sadie who came running from the kitchen.

"What is it, Master?"

"I'm dizzy. My stomach is cramping and I feel weak like I am going to regurgitate. Can you have Jacob go to Huntsville quickly and get Doctor Cartwright for me? He took me to see him once before, so he knows where his office is."

"Sure, Master Robert! I will ask him to go at once!"

Jacob took the surrey and was back with the doctor in less than an hour. Still Liz wasn't home.

"His condition is extremely mysterious," Dr. Cartwright told Sadie, Sally and Jacob. I haven't seen anything like it except from poison. Could he have accidentally ingested something harmful?"

The servants were silent momentarily.

Cartwright then remembered reading what had been reported in the newspaper concerning Jeffries' death, but was afraid to say anything further.

"Not that I know of, Doctor," Sadie finally said. "His wife is gone with some friends and we don't know when she'll be back."

Cartwright was curt with Robbie. "I am unable to stay. I have other patients waiting."

"What should I do?" he asked.

"Please drink a lot of water, Mr. High. And keep your head elevated."

"Yes, sir. Thank you. Am I going to live?"

"Only God knows. After your wife gets home, tell her to bring you to my office first thing in the morning. We have a special room set up where we can do some checking on what caused this."

By the time Liz got back that night, Robert was dead. Needless to say, he was immediately laid to rest in the family cemetery with no showing of emotion.

Soon after High's death, Liz's parents came to spend some time with her to help get her through her "grief." While they were still there, Liz filed a law suit against two of her neighbors, Abner Tate and Jacob H. Pierce, for $1400 which she claimed they owed her for her 1840 cotton crop. An action which High would have flatly refused to take.

Elizabeth swore under her breath as she read the letter she had gotten from Pierce.

*Madam, in the name of God, do you intend to try to ruin me? When I have protected your interest ever since the death of your late husband, Alexander Jeffries, in thousands of instances? Lest your mind should be treacherous, I will name a few. After the death of Mr. Jeffries, when his children should have been your friends, but instead of that, they were your most inveterate enemies and even went so far as to say you were the cause of his death, which was reported from one end of the county to the other. Who were your friends?*

Liz deliberated carefully about how she would answer. She didn't want Pierce to get hold of anything on paper that he could use against her in court. That Sunday she wrote her answer, but still didn't send it.

*I received your letter by father late on Friday evening, and company came in just at that time, so I had no time to write until I got home from church this afternoon. I am sorry to find your feelings are hurt with me, for I never intended to say or do anything to hurt you in any respect. Your kindness to me I do esteem in the highest, and ever shall, for I always have believed you to be my friend, and you may rest assured that I will not nor never intend to sue you...* (But she had just done so!)

Then she added the following postscript before having it delivered the next day by Jacob:

*I intended to have sent this last evening, but on account of Mary E. having a chill at church, it detained me so that when I was done writing, it was too late to send it. Then I thought I would get father to hand it to you in Huntsville, but finding you will be at home today, I will send it there. I hope all will be well yet. I am your friend: Mrs. High*

Upon reading her confusing letter, Pierce muttered softly, "With friends like you, who needs enemies?"

# Chapter Thirty-three

## January 1843: Hazel Green, Alabama

**A** driving, bone-chilling rain was slashing down on January 4th when Liz heard a rapid banging on the front door of her home.

"Liz, it's Barbara Hazel!"

"I know who you are! For heaven's sake, what's all the racket about?"

The drenched midwife shook herself off as she removed the soaked cloak from her head, dripping all over the floor. Her teeth seemed to be chattering.

Liz frowned.

"Okay, now you've got my dang floor all wet! So what on earth is your problem?"

"I had to talk to somebody. I couldn't just keep it all inside me any longer. Your neighbor, Abner Tate had a man killed in his house last month!"

"And you know this how?"

"I was there when it happened! I was working for him, watching out after a sick child. I was staying at his house and I heard it all going on during the night!"

"Who got killed?"

"Some fella named Rice who had a lot of money with him!"

"Who else knows about this?"

"Just his family and his servants, so far as I know."

"Well, has Tate done anything to make you think he's coming after you?"

"No."

"Well, since it's been a month or so, maybe he isn't thinking you're a threat to him. Sit in next to the fire. Let me fix you some hot coffee and I think you should just relax and let this blow over. Just stay here till the rain lets up. I'm having problems with Tate myself right now and I don't want him to get his nose out of joint worse than it already is."

"You really believe it'll blow over?" Barbara said, pulling a chair close the fireplace.

"You know what they say, 'Let sleeping dogs lie!'"

"I guess you're right. Thanks. You're a good friend, Lizzie."

After Barbara Hazel left, Liz shook her head.

*That Tate's a bad man, for sure; but she probably just imagined that. She's a nervous type.*

# Chapter Thirty-four

## 1844: Hazel Green, Alabama

"**M**issy Mary Beth is sick, Miz Elizabeth!" Sadie's soft voice was trembling. "Master William is outside playing. Missy didn't feel like going out with him."

Liz frowned.

"Where is she?"

"She's layin' down on her bed."

"Mary Beth, what's wrong, honey? How do you feel?"

"I'm hot, Mommy. I feel really bad!"

Liz reached over and put her hand on her daughter's forehead.

"Oh, my! You *are* hot. I'm going to take you to the doctor, Missy!"

"Sadie, get Joshua to hitch Blaze to the surrey for me at once!"

"Yes, ma'am!"

It was a sizzling hot day in early August. Liz cracked the riding whip and hastened Blaze onward to Dr. Erskine's office in Huntsville.

"Do you have a cotton crop on your farm?" the doctor asked.

"Yes, why do you ask?" Liz nodded and frowned.

"Has your daughter been around the children of your servants?"

"How the heck should I know?" My household servants watch after her! I can't be with her all day long! A lot of the time I'm gone with my friends."

"It would behoove you, madam, to know where your daughter is at all times. But you may be too late. Slave children are taking chills, pneumonia and fever, even in the summer time. These Negro children also spend time helping chop cotton plants and are exposed to disease-carrying insects, like mosquitoes. I fear that your daughter has fallen prey to one of these conditions by being with these youngsters. There isn't a lot I can do for her. Make sure she doesn't get dehydrated. Give her plenty of clean water to drink."

Liz suddenly remembered that Grace, one of the plantation slaves, and her mate, Aaron, had a young daughter to die about two weeks earlier who had been having chills.

"Yes, doctor, I will," she said as she paid the bill and started back toward home.

Sadly, on 13 August, two years after Robert's death, Mary Elizabeth passed away at home, only three months before her seventh birthday.

Liz was too embarrassed about the fact that she had not kept up with her daughter's whereabouts, so she told no one what Dr. Erskine had related to her. She remained out of the public eye, refusing to grant entrance to her home, even to her closest friends, before the funeral, two days after her passing.

William was deathly quiet and pouted alone in his bedroom.

Liz stuck her head in. "Son, I lost her too."

"I don't think you really love us, Mama! You're never here," he screamed. "Just go be with your fancy lady friends! Or that horse you love so much!"

Liz shut the door and walked slowly away. *What have I done?*

Rumors spread like wildfire around Madison County that the precious little girl had paid the price for her mother's darkness. Her tender body joined the growing remains buried in the family cemetery under the shade of the big holly tree.

Liz was trying ever so hard to keep her sanity over the next few months. She was looking for any spark of positivity that she could build upon.

Then that fall, from Friday November 1st to Wednesday December 4th the United States Presidential election was held—on different days in different states. When the votes were all tallied, Liz was thrilled to learn that Polk, who had organized the new Democratic Party, originally seen as a dark horse, had defeated the Whig candidate, Henry Clay. But then Polk had been supported by the powerful Gideon Johnson

Pillow, for whom Nathan Vaught had built Clifton Place.

*Money talks!* she figured.

Then she reminisced about what Robbie had told Polk about becoming President the night they had visited in his home and smiled. *That scoundrel was pretty smart after all!*

Liz immediately had Blaze tacked up, rode to the telegraph office in Huntsville and sent her congratulations to Polk's home in Columbia.

*Think about who I would be now if I could have caught James Polk!* Liz contemplated, as she leisurely rode back home. *I would have taken him away from that goodie-goodie wife of his if I could have been around him enough!*

With the limited money which she had retained after High's death, Liz impatiently ordered construction to begin on an L shaped mansion on the Indian mound in front of the two-story log house. But she knew before she even started that there wasn't nearly enough capital to build it. A lot of the crop money had been spent on Robert's failed reelection campaign.

She refused to acknowledge the fact that the sentiment against her had squashed any small

179

chance that Robbie may have had of being reelected.

Elizabeth continued her reign of terror against the frightened slaves, ruling them with a hand of iron. Anything to take her mind off of the fact that she wanted so badly to complete a mansion that she hadn't been able to wrangle enough money for out of her sorry husbands!

She would find a way to have her classy new home or her name wasn't Elizabeth Dale Gibbons Flanagan Jeffries High!"

# Chapter Thirty-five

## 1846: New Market and Hazel Green, Alabama

"May I help you, ma'am?"

"Yes, I'm looking for the store owner."

"It is I, madam: Absalom Brown! What can I do for you this fine morning?"

Liz had dressed very fashionably that January morning to go to the fancy dry goods store. But, like with most things she did, she had her covert reasons.

"I need some new bed sheets. My husband passed away four years ago and I haven't had the heart to change the bed clothes."

"Oh, I am so very sorry, ma'am! I have some muslin sheets, imported from East India. I'm sure that such a refined lady as you would want the very best."

"Thank you, Mr. Brown. That's mighty kind of you to say. But don't you have some simple cotton sheets made here in the States? Possibly in Alabama? I am a cotton producer and want to support our product."

"Hmmm, why yes! Of course, dear lady!" Brown was perking up.

"My young daughter also passed away two years ago. I would like some sheets for her bed as well. Oh, I guess you should just go ahead and get me some for mine and my son's beds while we're doing this."

"I will have them ready for you shortly, madam! Do you want plain white, or would you prefer a pastel? Perhaps pink for the female beds and light blue for the two male beds?"

"What does your wife prefer?" Liz knew full well that Brown had no wife. She didn't go shopping unless she had done her homework.

Brown's countenance dropped.

"My wife, God rest her soul, went to be with the angels five years ago."

"Oh, I had no idea!" she easily lied. "You have my deepest condolences. Just make them all white. My plantation is just a few miles away, between here and Hazel Green. I am sure you have been over that way. There are a couple of turns to make between here and there. I get quite lonely for some good company. You can't miss it, though. The house is on the left of the road going from here, on a large knoll. Please come by and visit me if you have a chance."

"Why, yes. I'm very familiar with the roads. I have seen your house up there, and your slave quarters when I have been on my way to Hazel Green."

Liz's parents had returned to Columbia, so she was now alone, other than the servants, and as free as an eagle in flight.

The distinguished 59-year-old New Market merchant was quite impressed with the sharp, beautiful, charismatic 51-year-old Elizabeth.

New Market was another small town just to the east of Hazel Green and it didn't take long for her to ride over to meet him and vice versa. Brown came by the plantation the next Sunday afternoon and Liz treated him like a king. They agreed to take turns with their visits.

Liz could have easily told a servant to hook up the surrey, but she much preferred proudly prancing in side saddle on her magnificent Blaze on a Sunday afternoon.

It wasn't long before she had Absalom believing that the whole thing was his idea and the two lonely singles were joined together on March 16th, with Brown immediately moving onto the plantation.

"What do you think of completing the mansion that I have started, Ab?" she ventured soon after the nuptials, pointing to the foundation stones and framed flooring.

"I think it's a grand idea, my darling!" Brown smiled. "We must get started on it directly!"

And so, they did. Brown could certainly afford the cost, as he had put aside a large portion of his profit for a number of years. The most fabulous materials were brought in from around the country. A slave carpenter was employed to undertake the massive project. Even with several able-bodied assistants it took them over a year to complete the stately mansion!

# Chapter Thirty-six

## Summer 1847: Hazel Green, Alabama

The home was built facing the east, because Liz wanted the sun's morning rays to greet the front of the house and the porch. This classy structure boasted eight huge, splendidly decorated rooms, including a grand ballroom, and had two majestic staircases. One staircase was in the front hallway separating the four downstairs rooms and the other was midway between the front and the back. The front foyer was moderately large, with a vast opening on either end.

The main front door was comprised of two large panels; at its borders there were miniscule glass panes. A very few feet from the north side, at the foot of the Indian mound on which it stood, ran the road from the village of Hazel Green, barely a mile to the west. This narrow boulevard was intersected a few hundred yards to the front of the home with a lane bordered by a dozen slave cottages.

A row of cedars and other evergreens encircled numerous beds of various types of colorful flowers and shrubs. Bear grass ran along the main walkway in front of the dwelling. Brick walks led around the mound, toward the stables and icehouse, skirted by other well-manicured shrubs.

The most elegant furniture available was obtained. Decorative servant's bells were placed in every room. But what made it even more special was the indoor plumbing. A bath and kitchen sink!

Still, Elizabeth was never fully satisfied. She envisioned lofty mirrors and extravagant mantle pieces. She never got those, however.

But Liz made certain that this grand home was not always a lonely abode surrounded by its curtain of elegant evergreens. Often guests would occupy its bedrooms for a night or so at a time when Liz gaily returned from Columbia with friends for her fancy house parties and other joyous festivities. The newspapers in and around Columbia hadn't reported the Huntsville gossip, so she felt more in control with this set of outsider friends.

This was well known to be one of the most luxurious homes in the county. Elizabeth was in high cotton! Pun intended. Her lifelong dream had become a stunning reality! She would be the envy of Northeast Alabama and Lincoln County in Southern Middle Tennessee which joined it on the north!

But what to do with Absalom now that the majority of his funds were expended? She had always gotten what she wanted; just as she had once told Alexander Jeffries, who had set this whole fantasy in motion. Well, she knew exactly what to do with Mr. Brown!

# Chapter Thirty-seven

## Fall 1847: Hazel Green, Alabama

In less than a month after their splendid new home was completed, the most unimaginable thing transpired! Absalom Brown took abruptly ill with a "strange malady" and endured a slow and painful demise which "caused his body to swell so that it was necessary that he be buried during the night of his death," according to the stories related by the slaves who were present.

The somber ceremony for Absalom Brown's funeral was held outside in the now notorious family cemetery on a dark and dreary night with lanterns being held by the servants. Faces were solemn; sweat was breaking out on the slaves brows in spite of the slight chill in the air. This time there were even a couple of neighbors present who were friends of Absalom.

Where have we heard this before?

Once again, a new, prosperous plantation master was badly needed.

# 1848

The next February, Elizabeth was introduced to another wealthy widower, Willis Roden Routt, originally from Kentucky, who was seven years her junior.

At this point, Liz wasn't particular. She needed a wealthy husband and Willis Routt was available. She had met him at her friend Anna's house and as always, had cast her wicked spell and weaved her silvery web around him.

Her magic was still working!

They were wed in an unannounced ceremony at a small Huntsville chapel on 11 May 1848.

# Chapter Thirty-eight

## December 5, 1848: Washington, DC

"**F**ellow-Citizens of the Senate and of the House of Representatives:

"Under the benignant providence of Almighty God the representatives of the States and of the people are again brought together to deliberate for the public good. The gratitude of the nation to the Sovereign Arbiter of All Human Events should be commensurate with the boundless blessings which we enjoy. Peace, plenty, and contentment reign throughout our borders, and our beloved country presents a sublime moral spectacle to the world...."

President James K. Polk was delivering his final speech to Congress before leaving office. It was with mixed feelings that he was wrapping up his stay in the White House. But his health was on the decline and he knew it was for the better.

# March 1849: Alabama

Polk had just left Washington in early March of '49. He and Sarah were making a long triumphal farewell tour through the South. When they arrived in Huntsville, Polk decided that they needed to make a quick stop by the old High plantation and pay his respects to the widow of his dear friend, Robbie. Late in the day of 10 March, near dusk, they rented a beautiful fringed surrey and headed out the few miles north to Hazel Green.

As the soot black horse pulled their surrey up the ancient mound, the ominous cry of a distant grey wolf greeted them. The crisp, full, worm moon peeked eerily through the drifting dark clouds and a bolt of rambling lightning split the early evening sky.

As Polk's large knuckles knocked on the huge portal, a bizarre chill ran down his spine which seemed to coincide with the alarming lightning bolt.

Sadie quickly answered the door, and her large, dark eyes opened to their fullest possible extent!

"Come quick, Miz Elizabeth! Come quick!" She was rapidly shaking both hands in excitement.

"E-e-e-e! Liz shrilly shrieked as she reached the door.

"Disappointed?" Polk said, smiling very slightly, trying hard not to laugh.

"Of course not, Mr. President! I just never dreamed in a million years that you would ever actually be showing up at my door! Come in! Come in!"

"I just wanted to reach out to you and express my most sincere commiseration on the loss of dear Robbie. I only heard about his demise right before leaving office. He was a fine friend to me for many years."

"Why, thank you, Mr. President!"

"Now stop calling me that!" Polk snapped, as he and Sarah made themselves comfortable in the richly appointed parlor at the entrance to the ballroom. "I feel the same way about that as I did when Robbie referred to me as 'Young Hickory' when I saw you last! Just call me James, like he did."

"Thank you, *James!* You know I always followed your every move in the *Huntsville Advocate*. And I sent you a telegram back when you were elected President, congratulating you. Did you get it?" Liz's head pushed forward.

"Yes, I most certainly did receive it! I still have it tucked away somewhere. That was very kind of you; thank you so much!"

"Oh, by the way, how rude of me! This is my new husband, Willis Routt!"

Willis was beaming.

"Hello, Mr. President! So delightful to meet you!"

"Likewise!" Somehow he didn't seem at all surprised that she would be remarried already.

"Well, I would love for the two of you to have dinner with us this evening," Liz said. "I will have Sally and Sadie cook us up some tasty Southern cuisine! And I would be most pleased for y'all to spend the night with us. We have plenty of room now!"

James and Sarah Polk glanced at one another.

"Well, I'm not feeling much like traveling this evening, anyway. We would be delighted." Polk nodded.

"Sadie, have Joshua unhitch their horse and put it in the stable."

"Certainly, Miz Elizabeth."

That evening they rehashed the past two times that they had met and Polk shared some intriguing stories of his friendship with Robbie when they were both young men. Sarah said very little. Polk asked to be excused early, due to his feeling poorly, and he and Sarah retired to the largest guest room for the night.

The next morning Polk was coughing profusely.

"We're on our way to New Orleans along the waterways," Polk said in a gruff voice, clearing his throat, "where we will have a large riverboat waiting for us. Then after we visit my mother in Columbia, we'll be settling in our new home that we just had built. We call it 'Polk Place;' it's in Nashville."

When the Polks got back to the hotel in Huntsville, where they had rented a room the day before, they were met by a local politician who had hired them a coach and come to see them off to their boat at the Coosa River.

"Have you enjoyed yourselves in our fair city, Mr. President? My wife and I were hoping to dine with you last evening, but we found that you had left town."

"So sorry that we were unable to make it, councilman. We went up to Hazel Green to visit Elizabeth Routt. She was married some time back to my good friend, Robbie High, who passed away."

"My, my! Yes, High was a personal friend of mine, as well. But Elizabeth doesn't have too good a reputation around here, if you don't mind my saying so. Are you aware that she is rumored to have poisoned her husbands?"

"No, I was not aware, councilman," Polk said in a clearly irritated tone, "but I don't put much store in rumors."

The councilman nodded and changed the subject. Going against the past President wasn't a good idea. Sarah's brow began to wrinkle, but she knew better than to comment.

After stops in Montgomery and Mobile then two along the Gulf Coast in Mississippi, with Polk not at his best, they finally reached the Father of Waters.

On the riverboat there, several passengers were dying of cholera and the President was vomiting, so the Polks disembarked and spent a few days in a hotel before completing their trip and settling at their new home. The doctor that he saw in Louisiana assured him, however, that he did not have cholera.

This visit was the last time that Polk ever saw his beloved mother.

Within a short while after getting to their new home, Polk once again began to take a turn for the worse. Consulting a physician in Nashville, the one whom he had seen while governor, he was told that he did have cholera now, and he immediately became confined to his bed. A full-time nurse attended him.

Though his dear wife and mother were both devout Presbyterians and he had attended a Presbyterian school as a youth, Polk had never joined a church.

In early June he summoned his wife to his side.

"Sarah, I would like for you to get John McFerrin to come and baptize me into the Methodist Church; after all, it was under his ministry that I was converted."

After his baptism, Polk's thoughts ran deep.

On 15 June, he and Sarah had their final conversation.

"Sarah, my dear, do you remember when I first started feeling ill this time?"

"Yes, my darling. It was when we were at Elizabeth Routt's home in Hazel Green, Alabama."

"You are so right, my love. You know how we were later told about how she was said to have murdered her husbands?"

"Of course I do."

"Well, don't you think it's a little curious that it was at her home when I started feeling ill?

"I never really gave it much thought."

"I love you, Sarah. For all eternity, I love you."

With those words, his spirit took wings.

# Chapter Thirty-nine

## 1850: Hazel Green, Alabama

**"I** don't fancy your parents staying with us indefinitely," Willis sternly told Elizabeth one bleak winter day in early 1850, as he prodded the fire with a poker.

"Well," said Liz, turning to face him, "They're getting on in years. They won't live forever!"

Willis frowned and sat down in his number one chair. "What's it been? Eight months now? I just don't like it one darn bit! There'll be worse problems come of this, you'll see!"

But Liz won the argument and nothing changed. As time marched on, the household slaves, who had been allowed to stay in the log cabin since the completion of the new house, could hear raised voices late into the night as they sat on the porch. They became very uneasy.

"Jacob," Sally said in August, "Things is really bad 'round here. We need to jump on that

Underground Railroad and get ourselves up North!"

"You's right, Miz Sally! But I's done got too old to make it. Miz 'Liz'beth would ketch me, and string me up or else shoot me, fo' sho! No, you go on ahead, Miz Sally. An' I hopes you makes it!"

"I can't go without you, Jacob! You watch out after me. I'll just stay here with you and we'll do the best we can!"

## 1851

Christmas in 1850 had been a lot of what we would call, "Bah, humbug!" Elizabeth could certainly relate to the saying, because by this time she had read Dickens' *Christmas Carol*. All of the slaves had been treated like dogs that wouldn't hunt.

In the spring of 1851, a young lady at church asked Liz about whom she had gotten as a midwife when her children were born, as she was expecting a child before long.

"A woman named Barbara Hazel," she told her.

"She doesn't live around here anymore. I was told by two different people that she has moved out of state."

"Hm-m-m. I hadn't heard that." *She must have gotten afraid of Tate for some reason. I wonder what happened!*

In the summer of '51 Adam began exchanging letters with a close cousin in Maryland who was asking him about his military record and details of his family history and genealogy. He was genuinely happy to have the opportunity to share! He loved thinking about those good old days of yore.

Tensions across the country, however, were already building because of ownership and mistreatment of slaves.

The correspondence was enjoyable to the aged Adam as long as it lasted, but his pleasure was short-lived.

In spite of his hearty health, on 14 October that year, the 83-year-old Adam Dale unexpectedly passed away. Like the denizens of the plantation who had predeceased him, he was buried in that ominous family cemetery. The cause of his death was listed as uncertain.

Polly wrung her hands in despair. Would she be the next to bite the dust? What had happened to her beloved husband? She was very unsettled and now mistrusted her own daughter. She had been hearing a lot of negative gab when she was out and about on trips to town in the carriage that Adam had bought from Flanagan. She also knew firsthand exactly how Liz had been treating those poor slaves. She would not stick around any longer to find out. She packed up her personal belongings at once and left within days, taking her carriage and most gentle horse, moving back to Columbia to live with her dependable daughter, Sarah, and her beloved husband, Nathan Vaught.

Another dark day came all too soon in Hazel Green. It was 16 December 1851. Only two months after the death of Adam Dale, Willis Routt also suddenly passed on. A quick death and hasty burial, reminiscent of Liz's other husbands interned on that cursed ground.

When Polly received the news of Routt's death in a letter from Liz, she was as nervous as a long-tailed cat in a roomful of rocking chairs.

She soon sent her son-in-law, Nathan, along with a helper from his construction crew, back to Hazel Green to exhume her husband's body and have it removed to what would become Rose Hill Cemetery in Columbia which Nathan would help to establish.

Polly knelt in the fresh dirt. Pushing up her long skirt, the dark reddish soil mushed into the lines in her old, boney knees. But she didn't give a care. Her husband's bones now rested in safe, close environs.

The look on her solemn face reflected the anguish in her sorrowful heart.

"Adam, I miss you so very much. I am dreadfully sorry for what has happened to our dear Elizabeth. She is not the innocent girl we hoped we had raised. But I know that you were ready to go. Rest in peace, brave warrior. I'll see you on the other side."

Polly stood and saluted the grave, while Sarah took her left hand and pulled her quietly away.

Being a fellow Freemason, Nathan took it upon himself, out of respect, to also move the remains of his fraternal brother, Samuel Gibbons, from the small church graveyard in Centerville to Rose Hill Cemetery. He instructed his Lodge to erect a fitting memorial with a Bible on top and extensive carvings, for which he paid.

But for the Machiavellian and unsuspecting Liz, her real trouble was just about to begin!

# Chapter Forty

## January 1854: Hazel Green, Alabama

"**E**lizabeth Routt!" Abner Tate called from the front of her elegant mansion, "You whore! How many times have I told you to keep your gol dern hogs out of my cornfield?"

Silence from the house.

Tate had left a good amount of his corn standing to pick during the winter for his own hogs and cattle. Three times he had warned her.

"If you don't take care of this immediately you'll be awful' sorry! I'll make you wish you'd never been born! Didn't you learn your lesson last year?"

"I'll get my bucks to fix that fence! I'll have them put rails at the ground level so they can't root under them. The ground is frozen now. Now you get the hell off my property! You mind your own damn business and I'll mind mine!"

The big hog lot was on the far east of the property, adjoining both the Tate and Townsend properties which were narrow on their west sides.

Just the summer before, the other neighbor, Darnell Townsend, had sued Liz for whipping one of his slaves for killing two of her hogs which had caused damage to his crops, but Liz was still hardened. She had fixed the fence then! And all she was being required to do now was pay a fine.

By this time, needless to say, a growing number of the good folks in Madison County suspected Elizabeth of killing her husbands.

Tate, being at the top of the list, didn't wait to see if she would have the fence repaired between their properties. Nope, he sure wouldn't do it! He decided to take immediate action. Yes, she was pretty. So what? She thought she was God's gift to men. Well, she sure as the Dickens wasn't! Tate didn't like her one flipping bit. The two of them just couldn't gee-haw.

It was January of 1854. Tate saddled his sleek Palomino stallion and rode to the Madison County Sheriff's office the very next morning. He would put a stop to this sorry, unruly woman no matter what he had to do. He was mighty proud of the Colt Model 1851 Navy revolver that he had just received in the mail from Connecticut and had it strapped on his saddle as he went.

Sheriff George Carmichael had his head lying on his desk, almost asleep, when Tate came barging in the door of the jail. It was almost 10:00. So far it had just been a ho-hum day in the big city of Huntsville. But that was about to change as Carmichael jumped up like he had heard a gunshot.

"I want to file a formal complaint against that bloody whore Elizabeth Routt in Hazel Green for murdering her husbands!"

Carmichael let out a hearty cackle.

"You and how many others, Tate? What proof have you got?"

"She has pegs on the wall in the main hallway near her front door where she has hung the hat of each of her victims after she killed them! She might as well have notches on a gun stock! You've heard what goes on up there in that big ole house! Everybody knows! Come on now, Sheriff!"

"That don't mean a dad-blamed thing! Go and get me some actual proof!"

"Just file my damn petition!"

"Oh, I will, Abner! For what good it'll do you." Carmichael shrugged, "But come back when you have something I can use to arrest her!"

Tate stormed out and burbled curses in harsh low tones as he jumped on his horse, dug in his heels and galloped home.

Due to a lack of evidence, the Huntsville Court had no choice but to dismiss the charges.

# *Chapter Forty-one*

## February 1854: Hazel Green, Alabama

"**J**acob," Elizabeth said one cold, heavily clouded day in February, "I have a nice tidy little job for you! I'll give you this brand new gold eagle to shoot Abner Tate dead. Fact is, I'm giving it to you right now!" she said, forcing it into his hand. "They're rare around here! You'll be the envy of all the rest of my servants—and the others around here. He's a menace to me and our way of life."

Jacob was deathly afraid of his violent mistress. That same day he took the coin to one of Tate's slaves named George and offered it to him. He didn't want to be the one to do the dastardly deed.

George shook his head briskly, handing the money right back.

"No suh re, bob! I hain't a-gonna do it! Not for all da money in da who-l-l-e wide worl'."

Jacob slunk slowly back home, trembling all over.

"I's damned if I does and damned if I doesn't!" he told Sally.

Sally began to sob. Jacob reluctantly took Liz's loaded shotgun and headed out, knowing that he was on a certain suicide mission.

Abner Tate was standing on his porch puffing his corncob pipe, the grey smoke encircling the faded brown cowboy hat perched askew on his head. When he had gotten as close as he dared, the frightened slave lifted the gun and quickly squeezed the trigger, hitting his target squarely in his pouched out stomach! Dark red blood gushed out and Abner Tate emitted a pitiful cry! Tate fell off the porch, landing hard on the frozen sod. Jacob ran away as fast as his pitiful old legs would carry him.

Tate's horrified wife bolted from the house and yelled at George to help her get him into the house.

Folding a large checked handkerchief, George pressed it on the bloody wound while Mrs. Tate ordered another slave to ride to Huntsville to bring Doctor Cartwright.

Johnny put a bridle on the first horse he came to, jumped on it bareback and sped away.

Luckily, Jacob was at a sufficient distance when he fired the gun that the shot was lodged about half an inch below the surface of the skin. When the doctor arrived, he removed the pellets, sewed up the wound, gave Tate a big dose of laudanum and told them that he was very fortunate to have survived. But survive he did. And he had gotten a good look at the man who shot him!

As soon as he was coherent, he told his wife to have Jacob killed.

"Now Abner, you know that would only make matters worse! I'll go to Huntsville myself and swear out a warrant against Jacob."

The terrified elderly slave was picked up by a pair of deputies later that same day. He never made any effort to deny what he had done.

"I sho nuff done it, Sheriff! I done shot Mista Tate! But I sho didn't want to! Miz 'Liz'beth made me do it! I's skert to death o' Miz 'Liz'beth! She'd a-done kilked me if I hadn't!"

In early March, Jacob was charged with attempted murder in County Court and sentenced to hang.

At the hanging, the next weekend, Liz was a no show, but a sizeable crowd assembled at the gallows to witness the hangman's pull. Jacob plunged into the hole below, writhing and jumping.

Immediately after Jacob's conviction, Liz was taken in for questioning. She naturally categorically denied knowing anything at all about Jacob's actions. Carmichael had no witnesses and no proof and was compelled to release her.

Prissy Lizzie thought she had it made, but she was dead wrong!

# *Chapter Forty-two*

## 1855: Hazel Green, Alabama

"**G**ood morning, ma'am! My name is Captain Daniel H. Bingham. I'm a military lawyer and teacher. I've been teaching school down the road in Meridianville this term."

Standing at the large half-open front door to Routt Mansion, Bingham removed his hat, and nodded.

"Meridianville, huh? My dearly departed husband, Congressman Robert High got that school started down there, and my son, William was one of the first students to attend there!"

"Is that a fact? You must be very thankful for his efforts."

"I certainly am! What can I do for you, Captain?"

"I'm investigating the disappearance of a dear friend of mine, Jonathan Rice. I was told that he was last seen around here somewhere back in late '42."

"I'm sorry; I don't know how I can help you, Captain Bingham. Uh, wait…did you say *Rice*?"

"Yes, ma'am. May I come in?"

"Yes! Oh, yes! Please come on in! I may be able to help you after all!"

"Thank you, ma'am!"

"Have a seat at the kitchen table. I'll fix you a hot cup of coffee. Do you want anything in it?"

"No, ma'am. I drink it black."

"You don't sound like, from the way you talk, that you're from around here originally, Captain."

"No, ma'am. I was born up in Vermont. I lived in Frederick, Maryland awhile after I was grown. I then started a military school for young cadets in North Carolina before moving down here to Alabama."

"Really? I was born in Maryland, but my papa moved us to Tennessee when I was just a young child, so everyone around here says I sound like a Southern Belle! Papa was a military captain, too. He was a leader of a band of young boys in the Revolution and commanded 100 men in the

War of 1812 and the Creek Indian War under General Andrew Jackson!"

"Very interesting! I know you must be very proud of your father!"

"That I am! How did you know this Rice fellow?"

"Well, you see, back in '38 I came to Alabama to accept a position as an engineer with the railroad. They were just starting to expand at the time. Jon Rice built me a carriage back then in Tuscaloosa and we became close friends. We had a lot of the same interests and did stuff together."

"You know, I believe that my late husband, Mr. Flanagan, knew this man, Rice, too. I seem to remember him telling me that he learned the carriage making trade from a young man named Rice."

"You don't say!"

"I think we might be able to be of help to one another. I know a woman who told me a story about a man named Rice being murdered. She was the midwife who delivered my children! Her name is Barbara Hazel. She was gone for a couple of years but somebody told me the other day that she had moved back to Hazel Green.

The lady told me where she lives and it's not too awfully far from here."

"And how would this be of help to you?"

"This fellow Tate, the one she says killed your friend; well, he's giving me the pure old devil! He's spreading horrible lies about me!"

"When can I meet Mrs. Hazel?"

"What would you think about going over there right now? I can have one of my servants prepare my carriage, or the surrey may be even better."

"That won't be necessary, ma'am. I'll take you in my buggy!"

After driving about 20 minutes along the main road and up a winding narrow lane into a wooded area of the county, they arrived.

"Barbara! It's Elizabeth Routt—used to be Jeffries then High, last time you saw me. I found out from a lady at church that you were living over here now. Luckily, I knew where this road is. I heard that you had moved away at one time."

"Well, hello there, Elizabeth! Yes, I moved to Mississippi. I hadn't thought about you in years!

Who's this good-looking fellow you've got here with you?" Barbara's eyes were sparkling.

"This is Captain D.H. Bingham, Barbara. He's trying to get to the bottom of what happened to that man you were telling me about that you said was murdered at Abner Tate's house. The Rice fellow. He wants to know all you can tell him about what you heard that night. You never really told me the whole story."

"Now you know I can't take any chances of him coming after me. That Tate's a really bad man!"

"That's the truth, if you ever told it!"

"I just need you to tell me what happened, Mrs. Hazel," Bingham said, "I'm going to try to put this man away where he belongs so he won't hurt anyone else ever again. I may even be able to get him hanged!"

"Well, I sure hope you can, Captain Bingham!"

Bingham could hear the skepticism in her voice.

"Well, I'm going to do my darndest, ma'am!"

"Yeah, well, that's what I want, so I reckon I'm gonna have to trust you. You see, I was working at the Tates' place back in November and December of '42. Mr. Tate introduced a young

216

man at the dinner table one evening by the name of Rice, who he said was from Tuscaloosa. After dinner both men retired to Tate's office.

"After settling Rice for the night, Tate came back in to tell his wife and me that their guest wanted them to look out after his money. I don't rightly know how much it was, but he had a whole lot of money.

"Later that night, I awoke to a powerful tumbling and scuffling going on in the office proceeded by screams of 'Murder! Murder!'

"I jumped out of bed to summons Mr. Tate and tell him they were killing someone in the office. About that time I heard Tate call out, 'Damn you! Stop that hallooing!'

"Then I heard a severe blow being struck and I heard a deep heavy groan and a sucking of breath. Like a dying animal; then someone said, 'He'll come to,' or 'Don't let him come to.' And someone replied, 'No! He won't!'

"Then another blow was struck, but lighter than the first; this blow sounded like striking an axe into the ribs or the backbone of a hog. I didn't hear anything else until Tate spoke and said, 'Well, Pleas, he held you or gave you a pretty good scuffle! Go out the gate, and if you don't think you can get it done, call Smart to help you, and George. Take your axe along, lay it in the ditch, and when you are done, wash, clean and lay it away.'

"The next morning I asked Mrs. Tate where Mr. Rice was and she told me that he left during the night. The slaves say that Rice was buried under the apple tree on Tate's property."

"Oh, my! That's quite a story, Mrs. Hazel! Is there anything else you would like to tell me?"

"Yes sir, there's more, alright! I might as well get it all off my chest! That's not the only murder that was done at Tate's place!

"On the 2nd of March, '45, I was visiting the Tate home. I hadn't heard from him, so I figured I was safe. While I was there, a man came by looking for John Gordon, a wagon driver from Cannon County, Tennessee, who had been working for Tate for nine years. The man introduced himself as Charles B. Sawyer, from Coffee County, Tennessee. He said that Gordon owed him money. They asked Sawyer to stay for supper.

"I went on to bed that night and didn't think any more about it. The next morning I smelled a horrendous odor. I wandered out to the old kitchen in the back and spotted Sawyer in the fireplace. His head was split wide open. His feet were resting against one jamb and his shoulders against another. There was an old Negro woman adding kindling to the fire in the act of burning him up!

"I went back into Tate's office and noticed that ink had been rubbed on the wall to try to hide the blood.

"I knew that that old woman would likely tell Mr. Tate what I had seen. I was afraid for my own life, so I moved to Tishomingo, Mississippi just as quick as I could and told no one what I had seen."

"My God, woman! Are you telling me the straight of this?"

"As God is my witness, I am!"

"I'm going to do some more checking on what you told me, but would you testify in court about this?"

"If you will protect me, I will!"

"Well, Tate will be in the custody of the law; I can assure you of that!"

As they drove away, Bingham stuck up a conversation with Elizabeth and seemed to notice for the first time what a true beauty she was. Perhaps he already knew, but hadn't made any reaction to her charms until he had been able to meet and question Barbara Hazel.

Liz saw how he was looking at her. His gaze was obviously one of admiration and desire.

She certainly knew how to take advantage of men. She would definitely play this for all it was worth to her greatest advantage.

Meanwhile, Elizabeth tentatively had a contract drawn up on19 November 1855 to sell her lavish estate to a neighbor named Samuel Rownsend. There was, however, the provision that he would pay it off within a reasonable amount of time, not to exceed two years.

But she waited in vain.

# Chapter Forty-three

## 1856: Huntsville, Alabama

"**M**rs. Sawyer, I'm Captain D.H. Bingham. I'm working on a criminal case in Madison County, Alabama. Your husband's name came up as being murdered down there. May I come in?

Bingham's first trip had been to Manchester, Tennessee.

"Yes, please. Do come in."

The attractive, well-groomed lady appeared to be in her mid fifties. She didn't act the least bit surprised at her visitor's words.

"When did you see Mr. Sawyer last?" Bingham asked as he closed the door behind him.

"I've been trying to locate my husband ever since he left here with a wagon full of produce and a large amount of money back in late February '45. He was headed to South Alabama. I have never seen or heard from him again!

"I got a letter about two months after he left from a man named Henderson McGowan in Memphis telling me a wild tale about Charles being murdered at the home of a man named Abner Tate down in Alabama. I had never heard of this McGowan fellow and didn't know whether to put any credence in that story of his or not! What should I have done?"

"Well, believe it or not, I have a witness who told me that is exactly what happened and I am bringing charges against Mr. Tate. Will you give me your power of attorney to investigate your husband's murder?"

"Yes, sir! I most certainly will! It would mean a lot to me to finally get some closure."

"Thank you, ma'am. I'll be in touch."

After Bingham got back into Alabama he went directly to Tuscaloosa and attempted to contact Rice's family, but had not a whit of luck. He was told by his previous business partner that the family had moved and left no forwarding address.

Bingham knew that he had no choice but to go forward with just the evidence he had already collected.

Once he was home in Madison County, Bingham filed charges in court against Abner Tate, John Gordon, and Tate's slave, George. All three were arraigned and bound over for trial.

The trial was set to begin Monday, 31 December 1855 and go through Friday, 4 January 1856. Presiding justices were M.K. Taylor, G.B. Strother, and G.P. Davis. Tate lined up an impressive defense team in the firm of Walker and Chambliss.

Captain Daniel Havens Bingham was the sole prosecuting attorney. None of the locals wanted to go up against Tate.

Barbara Hazel, of course, was Bingham's star witness. She testified for two days in a row, repeating everything that she had told Bingham. The shrewd defense attorneys kept her on the stand badgering her and making her anxious. They cut Hazel down at every turn, in an effort to discredit her, claiming that she was insane and deranged.

"But I have a letter here from a man in Memphis who wrote to Mrs. Sawyer telling her the same story that Mrs. Hazel has revealed to this court!" Bingham shouted.

"How do we know that letter wasn't written by your girlfriend, Elizabeth Routt?"

The courtroom erupted in clamor.

"Order! Order!" the judge shouted, banging his gavel rapidly on the bench.

Liz had shown up in court both days and Tate had set there, next to his primary attorney, steaming, watching her every movement. He had seen the eye contact between her and Bingham. He had already heard all the rumors. He was infuriated when he had found out about Bingham's infatuation with Elizabeth.

"That witch, Elizabeth Routt is behind this whole charade!" Tate whispered to Chambliss.

Chambliss nodded and smiled. "Don't worry, Abner, I've got this!"

Tuesday, on lunch break, Abner Tate, who was illiterate, paid an attorney named Col. Jeremiah Clemmons $500 to write a pamphlet titled *Defense of Abner Tate against Charges of Murder Pre-ferred by D.H. Bingham*. The two remained together after court until it was finished that evening and turned it over to a reporter of the *Huntsville Advocate* who printed it, inserting it in the next day's issue of the *Advocate* and the other area newspapers. It was the hottest item in print in all of Alabama!

In the publication Tate charged that Mrs. Routt's "bridal chamber was a charnel house."

"She is," he stated, "the woman around whose marriage couch six grinning skeletons were already hung."

Bingham had been so discouraged Tuesday after seeing the reaction of the justices to the defense that he was ready to throw in the towel. But when the pamphlet came out in all of the area newspapers on Wednesday, he was fighting mad!

*All is fair in love and war and this is definitely war!*

Tate was certainly blatantly condescending and sarcastic in his pamphlet. Enough so that sentiment was running high against Liz.

Chambliss took full advantage and read from it in court on Thursday:

"Poor soul – she is alone – she ought to have a husband, an industrious sober husband like D. H. Bingham. She has not been particularly fortunate in that respect hitherto, and in Bingham's opinion was entitled to all the consolation a sober man can bring to the bed around which nightly assembles a conclave of ghosts to witness the endearments that once were theirs, and shudder through their fleshless forms at the fiendish spirit which wraps the grave worm in bridal garment and enforces a lingering death with a conjugal kiss. The worst fate I could wish for Bingham would be the success of his undertaking, but I doubt whether the prize will ever be his. He is dealing with a shrewd, bad woman, and she may calculate that she can induce him to good endurance."

Again the packed courtroom was filled with noisy rumbles and whispers.

"Tate further says here," Chambliss continued in a plainly facetious manner: "I say for money, because I cannot believe even in him any amorous passion mingled with his feverish anxiety to get possession of the hand of Elizabeth Routt. He knew her past history. He knew that she offered herself as a reward to him only on the condition that he accomplished a murder. If he succeeded, every time her lips touched his, desire must have fled in horror, as if from the cold, clammy taste of a putrid corpse. He would indeed have waded through my blood, and the tears of a heartbroken wife and a host of agonizing relatives, to the possession of her property, but her person he could not touch.

*"The clasp of her arms around his neck would call*
*up dreadful shapes to sit upon his dreary pillow*
*And make his nights as fearful*
*As if the dead could feel the icy worm around*
*them steal, And shudder as the reptiles creep*
*To revel o'er their rotting sleep."*

Bingham was so angry that he couldn't see straight. He fired back by publishing his own rebuttal which appeared in the *Athens Herald* on Friday morning. He was determined to have the last word, and brought a copy of his article to court that day and read it in his close.

"You reverted to Shakespearean style poetry yesterday. Well, two can play at that game, old boy! I have composed an acronym to sum up this murderous, vindictive man:

**A**bhorred by God and man, still no pious thought
**B**rings repentance for the ruin he has wrought
**N**ot once the pangs of conscience has guilty soul
invade
**E**ven for the widows and orphans he has made
**R**epine in sorrow for the loved ones shyed,

*That name, that odious name! To every virtuous eye,*
*As the beacon of all scorn, will hang on high.*
*That body! Down to the dust! And it rots away;*
*Even worms will perish, o'er its poisonous clay."*

Chambliss arrogantly stood, his broad shoulders squared, for his closing remarks in the case:

"Mr. Bingham has failed but he deserves the possession of the venerable bride; I trust that happiness will not be denied him. The union is one so eminently fit and proper that it would be a pity to prevent its accomplishment. There is no crime, no vice, no detestable meanness that is not familiar to one or both of them, and though the dead should flee away in shuddering horror from the bride, there will be enough of grinning friends to witness the ceremony and congratulate the happy pair on this very day in 1856."

The court found Tate and his cronies not guilty. Elizabeth was so livid that she was fuming. It had come down to the most uncommon of conflicts: evil against evil!

Liz immediately countered with a $50,000 law suit against Tate for defaming her character.

# Chapter Forty-four

## Going Forward

**D**aniel Bingham was bound and determined to do everything in his power to win Liz's heart. At least Chambliss had been right about one thing, he reasoned: they deserved one another.

One day in early March 1856 Daniel was visiting with Liz, making casual conversation by telling her about some other unique feats that he had accomplished. Maybe understanding his many versatile abilities would pull her over the line.

"Back in '46 I oversaw the construction of the first franchise bridge ever recorded. It was called the Washita Bridge. It was one of the first covered bridges in the state of Arkansas, too. It was constructed over the Ouachita River at Rockport. I wish you could have seen it, Liz! It was so grand! Unfortunately, it was washed away by a flood the next year after it was built."

"I am surely impressed!"

In truth, she was letting Daniel's words flow over her like water off a duck's back. She was saved by a brisk knock at the door.

"Good morning, Frank, come in!"

"Good morning, Elizabeth, I trust that you are well."

"Yes, sir, about as well as any woman could be who has been dragged through the mud and stomped into the ground! This is my good friend Daniel Bingham!"

"Oh, yes! You know I followed the trial of Abner Tate in the newspapers. I didn't want to come around to talk with you as long as that was all up in the air."

Liz laughed. *Better to laugh than cry.*

"Daniel, Francis King here is my administrator, business advisor and bookkeeper. He handles my situations on the plantation and makes sure that I get what money is coming to me. We have some business to attend to, if you will excuse us, please."

The topics of their conversation ran from the money from the cotton crops to settlement of the Townsend suit and plans for that year's crop.

Bingham also heard some unexplained laughing. He twiddled his thumbs and kept his distance from the kitchen, but he was very uneasy and saw King as a threat to his relationship with Liz.

After they had completed their visit and Frank had gone his merry way, Bingham approached Liz with a look that made his feelings about the matter crystal clear.

"You don't need this Francis fellow for a cotton-picking thing! Marry me, Liz! My Anna died back in '51 and I haven't been interested in any woman since then. Not until now. I love you, Liz. I can take care of the business around this place for you and you won't have to pay him anymore!"

"Oh, Daniel!" Liz smiled and wagged her head. "I've been married six times and none of them went well for me. I appreciate you as a valued friend, but that is as far as it goes."

Perhaps she felt obligated to Bingham and didn't want to take the chance that he may fall prey at some point to the wrath of her demons. More likely, she had gotten all she felt that she could from Bingham and now it didn't seem like it had been worth the hassle of the chase. After all, he wasn't really rich.

But Bingham continued to pursue Liz and made no bones about it when talking to other people. Some folks spread the word around that he must surely have had a death wish.

Liz's law suit against Tate dragged on for the next two years and the 1858 Chancery Court record pointed to the suspicion which surrounded "Elizabeth High Brown Routt" and the mysterious deaths of her husbands.

A verdict had never been reached, but for the time being, she let it ride.

Rownsend failed to make good on his offer to pay Liz for her property, so she accepted a sure deal, selling her lavish mansion and estate to Levi Donaldson for $12,500, cash on the barrelhead. She let most of her slaves go with the estate.

"I'm moving to Chulahoma, Mississippi," she told Daniel Bingham one day when he paid her a visit. "I have some land over there. I'm going to take William, his new wife and my two personal servants, Joshua and Sadie with me."

The slaves who were left behind were very relieved. Donaldson wasn't perfect, but he didn't abuse them.

In early July of 1859, Elizabeth received a singeing letter from Sarah Polk which had been forwarded on to her by Levi Davidson.

*Esteemed Madam:*

*It has been a full decade since my dear husband went to join his ancestors. I have had no children to keep me company and I have given a lot of thought to what happened while James and I were at your home that evening not long before his passing. When we first arrived, some truly unusual things occurred. Most notably, James felt a deep chill run down his spine as we reached your home and he soon began to feel strangely ill. It was not long after that when he contracted cholera and left me here in this big house all alone. I believe that something on your plantation weakened him physically and heralded the beginning of the end of his earthly life.*

*I don't know what witchery you possess or what eerie curse resides there, but I want you to know that I hold you personally responsible for his untimely death. May God have mercy on your eternal soul.*

*Sarah C. Polk*

Liz frowned, tossed the letter casually into the fireplace where Sadie was roasting a young hen for dinner and went about her daily routine.

Soon William had also grown leery of his mother and removed with his wife to Memphis, leaving her unaccompanied to dwell with the ghosts of her past.

By 1880, they and their children, Percy, born in 1859, Eva, born in 1865 and Matt, born in 1866, had moved to Proctor, Crittenden County, Arkansas.

Liz eventually dropped her unwinnable suit against Abner Tate. It just wasn't getting anywhere and she was tired of occupying her mind with it. By this time, deep depression was viciously attacking her.

The outbreak of the Civil War on April 12, 1861 diverted the attention of the entire nation and no further charges were ever brought against the absent Black Widow of Hazel Green.

The war had a devastating effect on Liz and her once fabulous estate. Her Mississippi home had been burned by occupying union troops, leaving her to live in the slave quarters. Of course, she had no choice but to free her two remaining slaves, who were now aging, themselves.

Liz passed away in Mississippi on 7 May 1866 at the age of 70, lonely and comparatively broke. No memorial was left to honor the notorious memory of the "Black Widow of Hazel Green." The site of her grave is unmarked and even unknown.

Whereas she had been listed on the 1860 census as having assets of $116,000, the equivalent of $5,387,903.16 today; in 1870, after her death, her estate was valued at only a paltry $3,200.

Daniel H. Bingham died the following year in Tuscaloosa, where he was buried alone at a cemetery with the same name as the one in Columbia—Greenwood Cemetery, the oldest one in the city, where some very distinguished gentlemen were laid at rest, including U.S. Congressmen George Whitfield Crabb of Virginia, Marmaduke Williams of North Carolina and John Mason Martin of Alabama.

On 10 March 1869, Mary "Polly" Dale passed away in Columbia and was interned in Rose Hill Cemetery next to her famous husband.

Ghost stories continue to circulate of a ghastly misty female figure floating around over the broken gravestones near where the giant holly tree stood on what remains of the old plantation at Hazel Green.

At the same time, there have been numerous Nashvillians and tourists alike who have reported encountering the unsettled spirit of Sarah Polk haunting the mausoleum where she and President Polk are buried at the Tennessee State Capitol. Perhaps she is seeking in vain for the Black Widow of Hazel Green, whom she surely blames for the death of her beloved husband.

# *Epilogue*

Levi Donaldson's granddaughter, Zora Vaughn Rodgers of Huntsville, was married in Elizabeth's fabulous former home and Donaldson, himself, continued to live there until his death in 1874. The property was passed on to his heirs who kept it until 1902. From that time forward it was simply known as Routt mansion.

The house was eventually divided into apartments before falling into disrepair in the early 1960s; then burned to the ground in 1968.

Waylon Jennings' 1987 hit song *Rose in Paradise* written by Jim McBride and Stewart Harris was inspired by McBride's childhood memories of the tale of the Black Widow of Hazel Green, whom he mistakenly believed to be named Rose.

More recently, Bluegrass artist Shane Adkins wrote and performed a humorous ditty about this unforgettable legend.

The lyrics of the song "*One Mile East of Hazel Green*" by Shane Adkins recount the Black Widow lore, including this verse:

*"Six times she was wed at the altar of God*
*On her hands she wore six golden rings;*
*Now six men lie deep beneath the sod*
*One mile east of Hazel Green...*
*They say that six ghosts haunt the old plantation*
*searching for their fair but evil bride."*

Now there is one more song to her credit to be found on You Tube and Apple Music. It is titled *The Black Widow of Hazel Green* and it's on Jamie Bartlett's *Haint Misbehavin'* Album.

The cozy town of Liberty was hit by a tornado on the evening of March 23, 1889, which uprooted trees and caused extensive damage to homes. No fatalities were reported.

Long ago the town was separated from the well-beaten path by the development of a new straight State Highway 70 between Smithville, the DeKalb County seat incorporated in 1838 and Alexandria. Going there is like stepping back in time to the centuries of the past except for the use of motor cars and the obviously newer buildings. There are still only just over 300 residents and the simple life is still very evident.

Hazel Green remains an unincorporated community consisting of ten square miles with a 2020 census population of only 4,105.

Cotton still grows in season on the old plantation at the corner of Joe Quick Road and Jimmy Fisk Road which is privately owned and clearing has been done in recent years.

I visited it in March, 2022 and finding the remaining symbols of the bygone days are difficult. Not one of the stones in the cemetery is standing. Mysteriously, I fell flat on my face and tore my jeans soon after reaching to top of the mound. Some pictures are included here.

216 acres of the property was recently put up for sale, including the mound and cemetery, being offered for $6,480,000.

Nathan Vaught's Athenaeum is now all that is left of the women's college in Columbia. It is a historic site and a museum which is open for tours and available as a venue for special events.

Paranormal investigators believe the ghost stories and some who have gone to visit the site have left badly shaken. There is definitely something very abnormal about the old plantation at Hazel Green.

But, of course this story is all just a myth, isn't it?

No, I'm afraid not.

# *List of Real People*

## *and pages on which they are found*

## SLAVES

# Photo Album

# The Black Widow of Hazel Green

**Elizabeth Dale, the Black Widow**

**Adam Dale**

**2D 9**

**ADAM DALE**

The first settler (1797) in what later became DeKalb County, Dale built a water-powered log mill to grind corn for the settlers who followed him here in 1800. Traces of the dam remain on Smith's Fork, about 200 yards upstream.

**Historic marker now missing from the intersection of US 70 and Dismal Rd.**

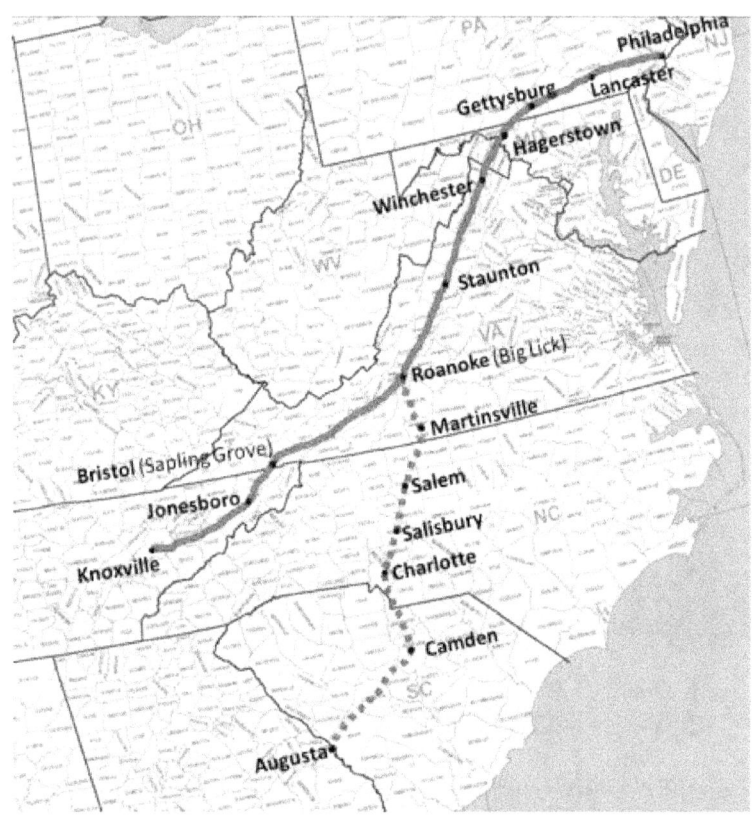

**Great Valley Road followed by Adam Dale**

**Route of the Nashville Rd., formed in 1788**

**Map of United States when Liberty was formed**

**Salem Baptist Church, 1919**

**Salem Baptist Church, 2022 (Photo S. St. Clair)**

**Salem Baptist Church Cemetery, 2022 (Photo, S. St. Clair)**

**James Brattin Gravestone, Salem Baptist Church
(Photo, S. St. Clair)**

**Samuel Gibbons Grave Marker, after moved to Rose Hill Cemetery, Columbia**

**Routt Mansion - Burned in 1968**

**Adam Dale's original stone at Hazel Green (Note incorrect age)**

261

**Broken Tombstones at Jeffries-Routt Cemetery**

**The Indian mound at a distance (from Jimmy Fisk Rd.)**

**Going up near the back of the mound (Photo S. St. Clair)**

**An apparent stone from the step to the house
(Photo S. St. Clair)**

An apparent piece of a gravestone
a good way from the cemetery (Photo S. St. Clair)

**Sign up in 2022 on property on Jimmy Fisk Rd. Hazel Green (Photo S. St. Clair)**

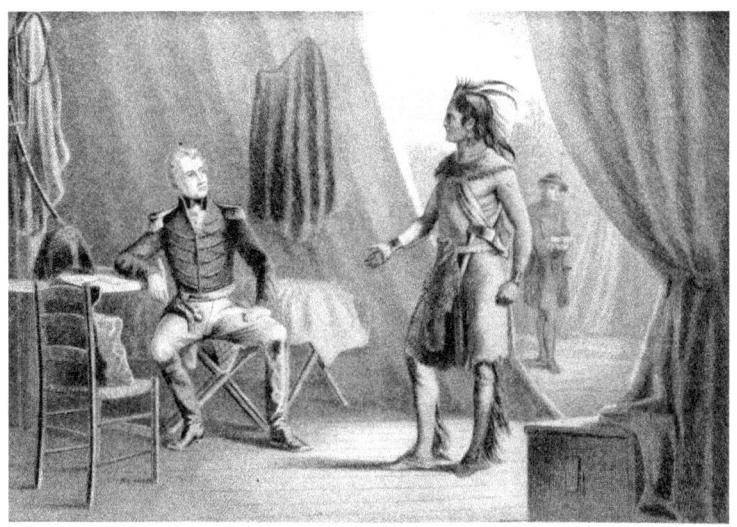

INTERVIEW BETWEEN GENERAL JACKSON AND WEATHERFORD.

**Signing of Creek Treaty, August 9, 1814**

CONSTITUTION HALL 1819

**Alabama's Temporary Capitol at Huntsville**

**Athenaeum Rectory, Columbia, Tennessee**

**Nathan Vaught constructed Manor Hall, Mt. Pleasant, damaged in March 2021 by a storm**

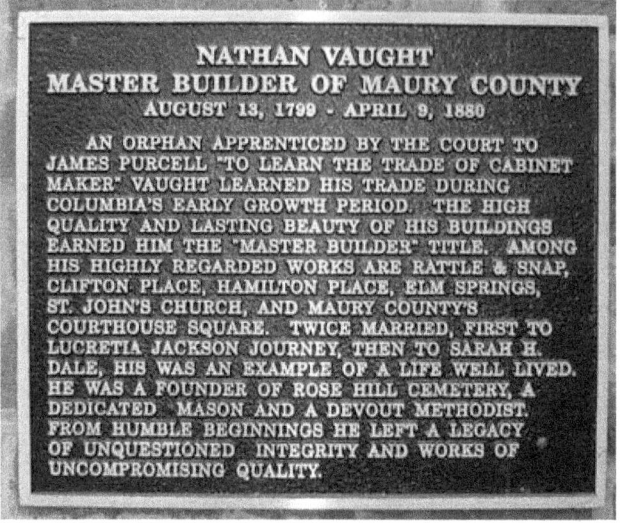

Historic marker in Columbia honoring Nathan Vaught

Nathan Vaught Grave Marker, Rose Hill Cemetery,

Columbia

**Rattle and Snap, attributed to Vaught**

**Elm Springs Mansion – Nathan Vaught (By rosograph)**
**Headquarters for Sons of the Confederacy**

**James K. Polk Home, Columbia, Tennessee**

**James K. Polk, 1849, Mathew Brady**

**Second Madison County, Alabama Courthouse, 1836**

**D.H. Bingham Original Military School Marker**

**Vance Co., NC**

The Black Widow of Hazel Green

# *References*

*Adam Dale photo* -Huntsville History Collection
https://huntsvillehistorycollection.org/hhc/index.ph
p?a=person&pe=Adam%20Dale

*Episode 62 of Southern Mysteries, January 20, 2020.*
This podcast, available on Apple Podcasts, was
created by Alabama native and Jackson, Mississippi
radio show host, Shannon Ballard.

*The Tennessee Genealogical Magazine: Elizabeth
Dale, 'Black Widow' or Unfortunate Widow*
https://www.tngs.org/resources/Documents/Maga
zine/Vol%2051%20No%201%202004.pdf

*Cotton Gin and Eli Whitney*, History.com

*Rock Island, Tennessee*
https://en.m.wikipedia.org/wiki/Rock_Island_Tenn
essee

*Post Offices of Smith County*
https://www.tnweb.org/smith/tngen/Poffices.htm

*The Nashville Road*
http://freepages.rootswen.com/-
tqpelfer/genealogy/Documents/Ancestral%20Migrat
ion%Archives/Migration5Webpage%20Folder/(3)%T
RANS-APPALACHIAN/Nashville%20Road.html

*Surveying - Encyclopedia.com*
https//encyclopedia.com/science-and-
technology/technology-terms-and-
concepts/surveying#~text

*Elder Cantrell Bethel:*
http://thehennesseefamily.com/getperson.php?pers
onID=16677&tree=hennessee

*Salem Baptist Church 175th Anniversary August 5,*
*1984*
http://sites.rootweb.com/~jmalone/salem175.htm

*Salem Baptist Church – Liberty, DeKalb County,*
*Tennessee*
https://www.tngenweb.org/dekalbtn/salem/salem.
htm

*County History DeKalb*
http://genealogytrails.com/tenn/dekalb/history.ht
ml

*DeKalb County - Tennessee Encyclopedia*
https://tennesseeencyclopedia.net/entries/dekalb-county/

*General Blue - 1830 Calendar*
https://www.generalblue.com/calendar/1830

*The American Historical Magazine*
Vol. 7, No. 1 (January, 1902), pp. 88-96
Rev. Thomas Craighead, by John O. Bass

*Legislation to Regulate Legal -Tender Value of Foreign Coins in the US- 1806*
https://www.usmint.gov/learn/history/historical-documents/legislation-to-regulate-legal-tender-value-of-foreign-coins-in-the-us

*Rock of Ages, Cleft for Me* – Augustus Toplady, 1776

*There is a Fountain Filled with Blood* – William Cowper, 1771

*Samuel A. Cartwright*
https://en.m.wikipedia.org/wiki/Samuel_A_Cartwright

*Friction Matches Were a Boon to Those Lighting Fires – Not So Much to Matchmakers*
Kat Eschner, *Smithsonian Magazine*,
November 27, 2017

*The Snow Hill Community* – *DeKalb County, Tennessee*
http://www.dekalbtennessee.com/snow-hill-community.html

*William Givan (aft. 1776 – 1822)*
https://www.wikitree.com/wiki/Givan-18

*Hazel Dale, Black Widow - Elizabeth Evans Routt*
http://www.geni.com/people/Elizabeth-Dale-Black-Widow/6000000018954196308

*Black Widow of Hazel Green Alabama*
Virgil Carrington Jones
https://digitalalabama.com/famous-legendary-and-notorious-alabamians/

*The "Black Widow" of Hazel Green*
https://www.google.com/amp/s/historicmaurycounty.com/2021/09/10/the-black-widow-of-hazel-green/amp/

*William Weatherford*
https://www.encyclopedia.com/history/educational-magazines/william-weatherford

*Duck River in Tennessee*
https://www.tn.gov/twra/fishing/where -to-fish/middle-tennessee-r2/duck-river.html#

*True Tales of Old Madison County*
The Haunted House of Hazel Green – by Virgil C. Jones pp 21-28

*Mystery of the Work Near Black Widow Gravesites Solved* **(WAFF 28)**
https://www.waff.com/story/24544477/mystery-of-work-near-mysterious-grave-site-solved/

*Moongiant* Full Moon and New Moon for July 1830
https://moongiant.com/moonphases/july/1830/

*District 2 Early Settlers of Hickman County Tennessee 1800s*
http://genealogytrails.com/tenn/hickman/earlysettlersdistrict2.html

*Tennessee Encyclopedia - Nathan Vaught*,
Richard Quin
https://tennesseeenclyclopedia.net/entries/nathan-vaught/

*Nathan Vaught*
https://findagrave.com/memorial/8219649/nathanvaught

*Nathan Vought*
https://en.m.wikipedia.org/wiki/Nathan_Vaught

*Adam Dale Vaught - PeopleLegacy*
https://peoplelegacy.com/adam_dale_vaught-706m73

*Columbia Tennessee, Historic Sites and Events*
https://duckriveragency.org/Rivermaps/Community/Columbia/Columbia_Historic_Sites_and_Events.htm

*Elm Springs House -* Wikipedia
By rossograph - Own work, CC BY-SA 4.0,
https://commons.wikimedia.org/w/index.php?curid=98722860

*Rattle and Snap*
Nathan Vaught with and for George W. Polk
U.S. Gov. - photo Public Domain, 1971

*A Brief History of the Cigar,* Aug. 21, 2003
https://www.actionnews5
actionnews4.ciom/story/a-brief-history-of-the-cigar/

*Arsenic: A Murderous History*, stiles.dartmoouth.edu

*North Carolina Education*
https://carolina.com'NC/Educarion/nc_education_vance+county.jtml

*Creek War of 1813-1814*
http://encyclopediaofalabama.org/article/h-1820

*Battle of Horseshoe Bend – Britannica*
https://www.britannica.com/topic/Battle-of-Horseshoe-Bend

*Photo: Jackson and Waterford; Creek War Treaty*
https://250yearsofmedia.weebly.com/1814.html

*Person: Adam Dale*
https://huntsvillehistorycollection.org/hh/index.php?/title=Person:Adam-Dale

*Edward Washington Dale (1790-1840)*
https://www.wikitree.com/wiki/Dale-2969

*When did "ain't" become slang?*
https://english.stockexchange.com/questions/196395/when-did-aint-become-slang

*History of the Madison County Courthouse and Bell*
https://www.huntsville.org/blog/list/post/history-of-the-madison-county-courthouses-and-the-bell/

*Politico: Tennessee enacted the nation's first prohibition law, Jan. 26, 1838*
https://www.politico.com/story/2012/01/this-day-inpolitics-071959

*James K. Polk Family*
http://millercenter.org/president/family-life

*James K. Polk: Life before the Presidency*
John C. Penheiro
https://millercenter.org/president/polk/life-before-
the-presidency

*March 1949- Moon Phase Calendar*
https://www.moongiant.com/calendat/march/1849

*Gideon Johnson Pillow*
https://en.m.wikipedia.org/wiki/Gideon_Johnson_
Pillow

*Explore Columbia, TN - Historic Athenaeum*
https://tnvacation.com/local/columbia-historis-
authaeum

*Alabama Sheriff's Association, Madison County*
https://www.alabamasheriffs.com/madison-county

*Clifton Place (Columbia, Tennessee)*
https://en.m.wikipedia.org/wiki/Clifton_Place_
(Columbia_Tennessee)#

*Huntsville History – Trail of Tears*
https://www.huntsvilleal.gov/historicmarkers/trail-
of-tears/

*Willis Roden Routt* (1790-1751)
https://ancetry.com/genealogy/records/willis-
roden-routt-24-1141llf

*Sketches of Prominent Tennesseans -* **William S. Spear** - 1888 Reprint, p. 154; E. S. Easley Southern Historical Press, Nashville, TN, 1978

**Colt Model 1851 Navy**
https://www.militaryfactory.com/smallarns/detail.php?smallarms_d=490

**The History Engine – Child Mortality on an Alabama Plantation June 25, 1846 – December 31, 1849**
https://historyengine.richmond.edu/episodes/view/4802

**Letter from Daniel Bingham to Adam Partridge**
2 March 1829
https://archives.norwich.edu/digital/collection/p16663/coll/id/16166/

**The Black Widow of Hazel Green – Haint Misbehavin'**
https://www.youtube.com/watch?v=Ckx5MW7mKT8

**Arsenic: A Murderous History**, stiles.dartmoouth.edu

**Cotton Gin and Eli Whitney**, History.com

**North Carolina Education**
https://carolina.com'NC/Educarion/nc_education_vance+county.jtml

*How 'Canon in D Major' Became the Wedding Song,*
Alexandra S. Levine, New York Times, May 9, 2019

*The Surprising Survival of Pre-Civil War Gold Coins*
by Brian Sweig
https://assetstrategies.com/the-surprising-survival-
of-pre-civil-war-gold-coins

*Daniel Havens Bingham (1802-1868)* Ancestry.com

*Daniel Havens Bingham*
findagrave.com/memorial/68670037/daniel-havens-
bingham

*Zora Langdon Vaughn Rodgers*
https://www.findagrave.com/memorial/10967871/
zora-langdon-rodgers

*Letter to Abner Tate*
http://libarchstor2.uah.edu/digitalcaaollections/ite
ms/show/3716

*The Alabama Supreme Court on Slaves*
https://www.lib.auburn.edu/archive/aghy/slaves.h
tm

*MADISON COUNTY, ALABAMA
LARGEST SLAVEHOLDERS FROM 1860 SLAVE
CENSUS SCHEDULES and SURNAME MATCHES
FOR AFRICAN AMERICANS ON 1870 CENSUS*
Transcribed by Tom Blake, March 2003

https://freepages.rootsweb.com/~ajac/genealogy/al madison.htm

*Okay, Listen Here! Five Southern Writers Have Their Say*
http://okaylistenhere.blogspot.com/2010/10/dead-husbands-tell-no-tells.html

*Mystery411.com*
http://www.mystery411.com/Landing_routtmansio n.html

*Jeffries Cemetery (Jimmy Fisk Rd.) Madison County, Alabama*
https://jparkes.github.io/smtc-website/AlabamaCemeteriesWeb/MadisonCounty/J effries-RouttCem/Jeffries-RouttListing.html

*Where Spirits Roam: Huntsville's Haunted Past* by Jacqueline Proctor Reeves

*Liberty, Tennessee*
https://en.wikapedia.org/wiki/Liberty_Tennessee

The Black Widow of Hazel Green

288

# *About the Author*

Stanley J. "Stan" St. Clair is a newspaper columnist for **The Southern Standard** and **The Smithville Review**, and the author of more than 25 other published books including the critically acclaimed series **Most Comprehensive Origins of Clichés, Proverbs and Figurative Expressions.**

He is also the sole owner of St. Clair Publications at http://stclairpublications.com. His articles and nostalgic poems have been published in numerous newspapers, magazines and books in the U.S., Canada and the U.K., and on several websites.

Stan served as a State Commissioner of the Scottish Clan Sinclair, U.S.A.; first for Georgia, then Tennessee, for several years and as its Eastern Vice President for two years. He was a regular contributor to their official publication **Yours Aye** for a number of years.

He is also a long time member of Kiwanis International, and has served in every position in his local club including several terms as president, and one year as District Lieutenant Governor.

Stan was knighted in 2003. He is an active Knight Lieutenant in the GPMTJ - Knights Templar of the United States, Priory of the Risen King, Commandery of St. Francis.

He studied creative writing at Tennessee State University and holds a BRE degree from Covington Theological Seminary. He was awarded an honorary PhD in 2020.

He is also is the co-founder of St. Clair Research, found on the Internet at http://www.stclairresearch.com with his distant cousin, Ad Exec Steve St. Clair, who owns and manages the project.

Stan was selected for inclusion in the 2022 *Marquis' Who's Who in America*.

Stan and his wife, Rhonda, live in Tennessee.